FALSE FATHERS

(WAXWOOD SERIES: BOOK 2)

TAM MAY

False Fathers
Waxwood Series: Book 2
Tam May

Published by Dreambook Press.

Click or visit:
https://www.tammayauthor.com

Cover Design © 2021 by Essi/100 Covers

ISBN: 9780998197968 (Print)
ISBN: 9780998197975 (ebook)

Quotes in the text are as follows:

Epigraph

Browning, Robert. "Pauline: A Fragment of a Confession." *The Collected Poems of Robert Browning*. A&L Ebooks, 2011. Kindle digital file.

Chapter 16

Shakespeare, William. *The Merchant of Venice*, Act III, Sc. V, l. 1

https://www.phrases.org.uk/bulletin_board/23/messages/847.html

Chapter 18

Shakespeare, William. *Othello*, Act I, Sc. III

https://www.shmoop.com/othello/iago-quotes-1.html

Chapter 27

Roosevelt, Theadore. *The Wilderness Hunter*. Standard Library Edition. New York: G. P. Putnam's Sons and the Knickerbocker Press, London. 1909. (Original

published in 1893). https://archive.org/details/wildernesshunte00unkngoog/
page/n10

To Aila and Becky for their encouragement and support of my work.

Then came a pause, and long restraint chained down
My soul, till it was changed. I lost myself...

— Robert Browning, "Pauline: A Fragment of Confession"

PROLOGUE

Want more feisty Gilded Age heriones who go against conventions? Love intricate mysteries with humor and a fun cast of characters? Then you'll love my free offer at the end of this book! So don't forget to check that out when you get to the end. Happy reading!

Go back, go back, go back, go back....

Malcolm Alderdice kept repeating those words. Jake heard it over the sound of the music rolling down the street outside. The band had wandered into Nob Hill's most lucrative section of Washington Street, as if to remind the wealthy inhabitants how much they owed their namesake, as it was Washington's Birthday today.

The wheezing voice drifted outside the bedroom where Grandfather lay dying. Jake and his sister Vivian sat as still as possible in the alcove where their mother had ordered them when the doctor arrived. "What does he mean, I wonder?" Jake whispered to his sister.

Vivian leaned her head back against the chair. "Perhaps — no, it's too impossible."

Tight creases around her lips and eyes made her look much older than her twenty-three years. Jake had seen those lines appear ever since she had gone to Waxwood four years before. Even now, as they waited to hear Grandfather's last breath, shadows were carved on his sister's face.

The wheezing words filled the alcove again: *Go back, go back.* The rhythm bounced up and down like the axles on train wheels. Jake recalled when Grandfather had taken him to see the trains departing from the Southern Pacific Railroad station for the first time. He had stared at the locomotive, hardly believing his eyes as he beheld its massive smiling grill. The locomotive advanced, and he covered his ears as it roared out of the station. Grandfather's eyes shone blue as he proclaimed, *That, my boy, was born of one man's idea. Fiddlers with life never have an idea. Remember that.* Jake would hear the ravings against "fiddlers with life" for the next ten years.

He looked out into the street. The band had moved on, but he could see their red felt hats and the gleam of their brass instruments as they turned the corner. His mother was always telling him, "Put it away and think no more about it." But who could forget the wheezings of a dying man?

"He's our grandfather, for God's sake!" He burst out "We ought to be in there."

"How sentimental you are, Jake," Vivian gave a morbid laugh.

He could not deny she was right. For weeks now he could hardly looked at Grandfather's emaciated figure without wanting to burst into tears. To watch the only father he had ever known spiral into uttering words with no meaning to anyone but himself had devastated him more than anyone else in the family, just as his grandmother's death had touched him the most. But it was not the Alderdice way to weep over anyone.

"Heaven knows where you got it," his sister continued.

"Grandmother was sentimental," he said softly.

"You mustn't think about what's happening in there." Vivian spoke in a softer tone. "What matters is what will happen afterward."

"How can you be so cold-blooded?"

"I'm realistic, Jake," she said firmly. "I'm worried about you."

A chorus of brilliant music still lingered outside the window, and Jake slammed it shut.

"You'll be twenty-one when our mourning ends," she continued. "Just the age to live."

"Yes, Mother mentioned something like that the other day." Jake grimaced. "She's rather pragmatic too."

"It's a serious matter, dear." Vivian peered at him.

"Must I think of that now?"

"I'm trying to warn you." His sister's hands reached for his. "Grandfather always wanted you to be the master of Alderdice Shipping and Alderdice Lines."

"He told me," Jake murmured, digging his hands into his knees.

"You don't want to be a shipping tycoon, do you?" She was still peering at him. "You want to be an artist."

"I don't want to think about it now."

"You must tell Mother," his sister insisted. "Jake, promise me you'll tell her."

"All right, all right!" His raised voice sounded like shouting in the muted alcove. "Leave me alone now."

The door to their grandfather's room opened. The wax-like features of their mother's countenance that had been steady for weeks were now melted. The doctor stepped out, his face grave. "You may go in now," he announced. "But only for a few moments. We don't want to tire him."

"Would it really matter now if we did?" The lines around Vivian's mouth and eyes returned.

Grandfather looked like a doll lying in bed surrounded by

cushions and blankets. The chair nearby was high and wide, the bureau massive. Jake felt as if he were Alice looking into the abyss of the gigantic room.

Grandfather raised his head. "Rain, rain!" he pointed at the window.

Jake gazed at the decapitated houses on Washington Street. Grandfather had built Alderdice Hall on the hill towering above the others.

Vivian said in a harsh voice, "There is no rain, Grandfather."

"Eh?"

"There is no rain!"

He blinked at her for a few moments. Then, calmer, he said, "Close the shutters, will you, my boy?"

Jake did as he was told. With only the gaslights, the room had an eerier glow.

"No rain now," Grandfather said, contented. "But, ah, the sea, the sea! The sea drops, you know."

"Drops, sir?"

"Hush, Jacob," Larissa whispered.

"Into the bay, of course." He stared at Jake with vacant eyes. "Penelope used to draw fish. I'd hold 'em down, and she'd draw 'em."

From the corner of his eye, Jake saw his sister stiffen.

"Always liked those fish." Grandfather lamented. He raised a shaking hand at Jake, and Jake took it. "You, you never draw fish, do you, my boy?"

"She wanted me to draw trees, sir." Jake smiled.

"Nineteen now, aren't you? I was fourteen." His grandfather pointed a finger toward the sky.

"You mean you were fourteen when you became head of the family, don't you, Grandfather?"

"Fourteen." The man's eyes shown like sapphires. "Make them proud, my boy."

"I shall make you proud."

"Not me! Them, them!"

Jake gut tightened like a fist. *Them.*

The finger now pointed at Jake. "Be no fiddler with life."

"I won't be, sir," Jake insisted.

"When one stands at the gates of Heaven, my boy, one sees how precious life is."

Jake pressed his lips together as hard as he pressed the old man's hand.

"They're watching you, always watching. You remember, my boy?"

Jake's heart pounded. "I remember."

"It's the men who must bring honor to the family. The men!"

"And the women, Grandfather?" Vivian's voice beat into the quiet room. "We can bring honor too."

"The *men*!" He shouted. "The women make the men who bring honor." He burst out with a roaring laugh, the one Jake remembered as a child. Then his grandfather's shoulders slumped, and he looked half his size under the thick blankets.

"Ought to have done better with the boy, Risa." He looked at her. "Ought to have taken him more in hand."

"Please don't, Father!" Larissa cried.

He sighed. "Poor Risa. Two husbands and fiddlers with life, both of 'em."

Jake met Vivian's eyes. They had never heard their grandfather refer to their fathers in this way.

"*Go back, go back,*" Grandfather wheezed. He became forceful, resolute as in the days before his illness. "We must go back, Risa."

"Go back where?" Jake asked.

His mother shot him a look, and his sister bit her lip.

"Mustn't linger, fiddler, no, no." Grandfather raised his finger now at Vivian.

Vivian replied, "I don't intend to."

He cleared his throat. "Risa, see that she marries. A good one this time who won't go running off to climb mountains and such nonsense. No more running off in this family!"

The fire in Vivian's eyes told she was about to remind their grandfather her husband had been an explorer and had not gone "running off." He grabbed her hand, silencing her in time.

"And you, my boy!" Grandfather wheezed. "Don't be like the others." He leaned forward, the thick blankets falling from his chin.

"I've never been like them." Jake fought to keep his voice from breaking.

"You and Mother made sure he wouldn't be," his sister snarled.

"Vivian," Larissa hissed.

His grandfather burst out laughing. "Honest, like her grandmother!"

"Honesty over frippery, isn't that right, Grandfather?" Vivian eyed him. The words made Larissa turn pale.

He gazed at his daughter. "I did her wrong, Risa. Only you know how I did her wrong." His head lolled to the side. "But I shall make amends now I'm going to be with her."

"Don't fret, Father." Larissa petted his hand.

"I shall make amends." He regarded Jake with a soft look. "Man's got to find his place, or he ends up fiddling with life."

"Yes, sir," Jake murmured.

The man leaned back with a smile. "Penelope will approve. Yes, she will approve in the end."

Vivian's lips were narrow. He knew she was remembering Grandmother's words to their mother: *Don't lock Jake in your cage of propriety, Larissa. He's not that way.*

Grandfather grasped Larissa's hand, his face relaxed with the self-assurance that had made him a leader of Washington Street society. "We'll go back one day, my darling. I promised you we would go back, didn't I?"

Jake realized he was seeing Larissa as a haunted image of the wife he had lost four years ago.

"Oh, it was unpleasant, I grant you," Grandfather continued. "*He* was to blame for that." A sound escaped from Vivian's throat. "But one can erase a tragic summer, can't one?"

Vivian opened her mouth but Larissa's glare was so vicious, she suppressed the retort and looked away.

"You and I were different from the others. ," he lamented. "We knew what we had to do."

Larissa smoothed down the covers with jerking hands, remaining silent.

"You and I were always honest with one another, eh, Penelope?" He looked right through her. "Honesty is the Alderdice way."

Jake turned to his sister, his eyes wide. She was laughing. She was genuinely laughing as she had not done for months.

"Get out, Vivian." His mother growled.

"No, no!" Grandfather said. "Let her stay. She's the honest one. Let her stay." The dreamy voice ceased, replaced by command. "We must both make amends now, Risa."

"We will, Father," said Larissa. "Rest now."

His grandfather sank back with a satisfied sigh. "When we go to Waxwood, it will be all right again, Penelope." He closed his eyes, a contented smile on his lips. "I will show you our Risa is a true Alderdice. As true an Alderdice as ever lived, eh?"

His mother motioned for both of them to leave the room. Jake watched as Larissa sank into a chair and took his grandfather's hand. She bent forward, speaking softly to him as a mother would to a troubled child.

The moment he was out of the room, sobs flew from of his throat. He ran to his room where the thick walls absorbed his wailing sounds. He emerged what seemed like hours later, his face hot and swollen. He found his sister in the parlor, her eyes dry, her lips strung tight in a thin line.

CHAPTER 1

Grandfather died that same night in a fury of wheezing words. The funeral was as elaborate an affair as Grandmother's funeral had been four years before. Larissa's devotion to him had been so great that she went into deep mourning for a full two years. She kept the house shrouded in black, the curtains drawn beyond what even Washington Street society considered appropriate.

For a long time, Jake could do little more than scribble in his sketchbook. As his pain eased, he could draw a coherent picture. Larissa permitted Vivian to go out on walks, but only with an escort, so he accompanied her during the late morning hours when there were fewer people about.

The day after the mourning ended, the curtains were drawn around the house. Alderdice Hall appeared luminous and airy again, the sun throwing patches of warmth onto the hardwood floors. As he dressed, his feeling of freedom turned into apprehension. He heard Vivian's words: *You must tell Mother.* He had turned twenty-one a few months before. Today was the beginning.

When he entered the dining room for breakfast, he found

Larissa and his sister at their usual places, as if the two years in black had never been. His mother looked composed and detached in navy blue suit.

"Mother, you ought to wear cornflower blue." He greeted her with an airy peck above her cheek. "It's all right now, you know." He took his place beside his sister.

"That is no longer your place, Jacob," Larissa said. "You sit at the head of the table now."

He shrank back, staring at the chair elevated with cushions that had been his grandfather's.

"You're going to force him to sit in a dead man's place?" His sister stared.

"I don't intend to force him to do anything. I merely expect him to do his duty."

He removed the cushions and sat down. "Haven't I always done my duty?"

"I have no complaints against you on that score," she agreed.

"The implication being you have complaints against me," Vivian said with a wry smile. "Obedience was never my strong point, was it, Mother?"

Larissa gazed shrewdly at his sister. "Only recently, dear." Vivian looked away. His mother continued as he unfolded his napkin. "There are certain things we must discuss."

"Now that it's all over?" He licked his lips.

"All over with?" Larissa took up a cream-colored envelope that had come with the morning mail.

"Now that we can get on with our lives," Vivian said.

Larissa glared at her. "That's hardly respectful, Vivian."

"I'm only trying to be honest," she said. "Just like Grandmother was."

"There is such a thing as brutal honesty, Viv," Jake pointed out. "It's not very appropriate under the circumstances."

"Very true, Jacob." His mother gave him a satisfied look.

"But he's dead," Vivian said. "Surely, we're permitted to say the word now, just as we're permitted to wear bright colors and greet the sun."

Larissa's knife came crashing down on the floor. Basset, their butler retrieved it and returned to his place against the wall as discreet as ever.

"I'm sorry, Mother." Vivian paled. "I don't wish to upset you this morning."

"Vivian is only concerned for me, Mother," he said. "We never really discussed what would happen when I turned twenty-one."

"I suppose your grandfather didn't think—" His mother took a deep breath before continuing, "He told me several times how happy it would make him if you were to take your place in the business when you came of age."

"Don't you think it's a rather heavy burden to put an entire empire on a nineteen year old's shoulders?" Vivian asked.

"Your brother realizes he has a responsibility to the family."

Jake placed scrambled egg on his plate, but he had lost his appetite. "I wasn't intending to flounder about, Mother."

"I didn't think you were," she said. "And I didn't intend to put the entire empire on your shoulders, as your sister so picturesquely puts it." She gave his sister a shrewd look. "You shall begin at the beginning, just as your grandfather did."

"I respect Grandfather's wishes," said Jake. "But I don't think I would be good at business."

"Well, then?" She looked at him.

"I want to paint."

"Paint!"

"I mean I want to be an artist," he corrected. "A professional, successful, and *respected* artist"

He expected his mother to reject the idea, but she looked interested. "How do you expect to go about it?"

Her seriousness filled him with hope. "I'm not sure yet."

"Jake hasn't exactly had the chance to consider it," Vivian

snapped. "We've all been locked up in this house, or have you forgotten, Mother?"

"I intend to devote this summer to finding out," he promised.

Larissa threaded her hands together. "I'm not entirely opposed to the idea, as long as you are respectable."

"I don't plan on disgracing the family," Jake mumbled.

"I just want to make sure you know what's expected of you, Jacob."

His sister let out a sour laugh. "Good Lord, you've been doing nothing but laying down expectations since we were born!"

"Those were the expectations of children," said Larissa. "Neither of you are children anymore."

His eyes fell on his sister. Vivian's summer green muslin suited her perfectly, but the shade of strawberry blond was duller than it had been four years ago. If his own mourning had strangled him, he could hardly imagine hers — two years for Grandfather, and before that, two years mourning her husband.

Larissa reached for the toast. "We must take our proper place in society again. All of us." She glanced at Vivian.

His sister did not shy away from the implication. "I suppose you're going to say my proper place is to marry again." She set her cup in the saucer, a little too hard. "Perhaps you've forgotten, Mother, but I'm no longer a belle. And everyone knows it, despite your insistence that I go by Miss Alderdice and not Mrs. Caulfield."

"Really, Vivian," his mother mumbled. "A widow ought to marry again."

"Not always," Vivian said with a grimace. "She might take up little orphans or write letters to comfort the insane."

"This is no joking matter!"

"And my place?" Jake asked, his throat dry.

"Yours is to make your contribution to the family honor," said his mother. "Just as every male member of this family has."

"You sound as antiquated as Grandfather," Vivian remarked. "These days daughters can contribute to the family honor too."

"You don't understand, Viv," Jake breathed. "You don't know."

"That's right, dear," said his mother. "You don't know." She then turned to him. "I don't want to discourage you, Jacob, but I do wish you would consider other options before you decide."

"Such as?"

"Alderdice Shipping, of course," Vivian snorted.

Ignoring this, his mother continued, "I realize many young men with a solitary nature such as yours turn shy away from business—"

"I know I'm the odd duck in our set because I have no interest in business or sports like other young men," he said warily. "But society has its artists too."

"Jake has always been serious about his painting, Mother," Vivian added.

"Have I ever behaved as if he weren't?"

"No, but you've never encouraged me either," Jake said. "I need encouragement if I am to make something of myself as a painter." He looked at her with pleading eyes.

"Well, it's a shame you have no interest in the business." Larissa sighed. "Alex Runyan has been ready to teach you for years."

He felt his breath catch in his chest. "I can't be who I'm not."

"I don't ask you to be." His mother rung the bell. "Well, if that's your decision, so be it. You shall have the summer by the beach to make your plans. We all need a change from the city."

"Where are we going?" Vivian asked.

Basset entered the room, and Larissa gave him instructions. After he left, she refilled her coffee without looking at either of them, "To Waxwood, of course."

Vivian dropped the knife in her hand. Jake understood his sister's reaction. When Bertha Ross had come to his grandmother's funeral, uninvited and even forbidden, Larissa had pushed away all discussions of Waxwood.

"I thought you hated the place," Jake said.

"I never said I hated it," his mother objected. "The mention of it always upset your grandfather, that's all."

"The mention of it upset you too," his sister pointed out.

"He wanted you both to see it," said Larissa in a soft voice. "He said as much, remember?"

His grandfather's words that night grated like a saw on wood: *We must go back. We must make amends.*

"You're taking the ramblings of a dying man to heart?" Vivian peered at her.

"I thought you of all people would be pleased."

"I don't know if 'pleased' is the word," Vivian mumbled.

"I believe it's quite a resort town now, isn't it?" Jake hoped he sounded enthusiastic.

"I imagine it's changed since your sister was there." She was looking at Vivian as if to remind her of the day she had run off to Waxwood without permission, still dressed in weeds from their grandmother's death.

Vivian caught their mother's eye. "Are you really taking us because Grandfather wanted it?"

"It's bad luck not to fulfill a dying wish, dear."

"You always said superstition could never touch the Alderdices," his sister reminded her.

"Superstitions and bad luck are not the same," Jake pointed out.

"Indeed they are not," Larissa agreed.

"Do you know why he asked us to go? The real reason?"

"He wanted to make amends," Jake murmured. "What sort of amends and to whom, we don't know."

"I know," said his sister. "He knows he would never live to make amends, so he wanted us to do it for him."

"It was a dying wish, Vivian," his mother insisted. "Don't make more of it than that."

"He was always making others do what he hadn't the courage to do himself."

"I won't permit you to speak of your grandfather that way!" Larissa snapped. "As your brother pointed out, it's a rather popular summer place. Ezra Wingham took his bride there only last year, and the Griffiths mentioned they might go this summer." She put the napkin on the table, signaling the end of breakfast. "We all need the rest."

Vivian rose. "Suppose I won't go?"

"I won't permit you to stay here alone." Larissa's voice was firm. "Why, the neighborhood will be deserted."

"I don't care," said his sister.

"You're being childish about this, Viv," Jake said.

"I'm afraid, dear."

"There is nothing to fear," Larissa said firmly.

"There is always something to fear," Vivian said, "when there's a chance of reviving a specter."

His mother rose, the blue in her eye as sharp as the blade of a knife. "I thought we went through all that a long time ago."

"Specters never really die, Mother," said Vivian. "They can emerge again."

"Only if you let them," Jake mumbled.

His mother left the dining room. His sister turned to the mirror on the wall, her eyes lost. He wondered whose reflection she was really seeing.

CHAPTER 2

The train station swarmed with people of all classes eager to begin their summer vacation. After two years of isolation, the sight of so many people set Jake's nerves on edge. He secured Vivian's hand under his arm as his mother sent a station agent to get their tickets.

Larissa, too, seemed intimidated as she secured the pins on her hat. "I don't think we shall have much trouble over the seats," she said over the noise.

"We're not going in the private car?" Jake asked.

"We've been away from society for too long," his mother said. "Though I would hardly call *this* society." She gazed with distaste at a people around them.

"We couldn't remain shut in our little world forever, could we?" Vivian pointed out.

Larissa gave her a fierce look. "I never implied we should."

The station agent returned with the tickets and pointed out the parlor car already waiting at the end of the platform. It stood majestic and removed as when Jake had first seen the trains as a child. Vivian murmured, "The Bowline Express. It's *déjà vu*, always *déjà vu*."

Larissa peered through the train windows as Jake and Vivian settled into the plush green seats. "The Griffiths said they were taking this train."

"They're probably decided to use their private car," said Vivian. "They would condescend to sit with us."

"The Griffiths have always been generous," her mother replied in a stiff voice.

At that moment, a woman rushed into the car in a flurry of scarves and books. Claiming one of the seats, she scattered the books and scarves, tipping her hat in the bargain. The intelligent features revealed the woman to be Marvina Moore.

Jake could not help but smile at the annoyed look on his mother's face. Vivian delighted at the sight of her, as they had become good friends, much to Larissa's disapproval. Mrs. Moore was middle-aged, a widow, and came to Nob Hill from some social wasteland in the southern part of the state. As of late, she had earned the dubious distinction of being a "blue-stocking" and an endless source of gossip for Washington Street matrons.

"Good to see you all in the light of day again." Her voice was loud but sincere. "I always regret we have such lengthy mourning practices. I don't know that even Queen Victoria is so tied to her weeds anymore." She greeted him with an amiable smile and nodded at Larissa.

His mother's arched her eyebrows. Washington Street knew Mrs. Moore had refused to go into mourning after her husband died and boldly appeared on the street the day after his funeral in cherry red.

"You're off to Monterey for the summer?" Vivian took the chair beside her.

"No, you'll never guess where." She looked at Vivian with some satisfaction. "I'll be spending my summer in that dismal little town of ours with the wax wood trees. Remember?"

Jake caught the flush in his sister's cheeks. "So are we."

"What do you call it, 'that dismal little town of ours'?" Jake asked.

"We talked about Waxwood when we took the train there a long time ago," Vivian said quietly.

"Not so long ago," said Mrs. Moore. "Six years now, I think. Oh, it was quite a different place then." Mrs. Moore leaned back with a sigh. "Did you know Brandywine is no longer there?"

His sister was silent for a moment. "No. I didn't know."

"Oh, yes, it seems the artists left some time ago, however little of them there were."

"Poor thing," Vivian murmured.

"What?" Mrs. Moore asked as she slipped a lorgnette out of her bag.

"Nothing."

The woman turned to him, smiling. "Are you still painting, Jacob?"

"Call him Jake," Vivian said. "Only Mother calls him Jacob."

"Then you shall call me Marvina," she insisted.

"Yes, ma'am," he said. "To both."

"You're staying at the Waxwoodian, Larissa?" Marvina glanced at their mother, who responded with a curt nod.

"You too?" Vivian smiled. "We shall not be alone, then."

"I'll make sure you don't become like Anna Karenina." The widow laughed. "We shall see something of your work this summer, Jake?"

"My work?"

"Your paintings, of course," said Marvina. "Vivian says you've been rather exclusive about them."

Jake blushed. "I prefer not to boast about my paintings before I'm sure there is something to boast about."

"Then you must be very good," said the widow. "Every bad artist I know shouts in everyone's ear about his work."

"Oh, you're acquainted with artists?" Larissa now joined the conversation with some interest.

"Marvina belongs to the San Francisco Arts Club, Mother," said Vivian.

"Not a very lucrative place," she admitted. "Those of us with a little money to spare and a grave appreciation for the arts find some interesting people there, not to mention some very talented artists."

"Mutual advantages to both parties, I'm sure." Larissa's eyes searched the platform. Jake knew she was looking for the Griffiths.

"We ought to make a very cultured party," said Marvina. "Vivian and I with our books and you with your paints." Her eyes slid toward Larissa."It's a shame you have no love of music or dance, Larissa, or you might complete our jolly little company."

"Mother's talents lie elsewhere," Vivian remarked. "She gives orders beautifully."

His mother scowled, but it was so subtle, it looked more like a quiet frown.

"Perhaps we can get your mother interested in something this summer." Marvina patted her hand. "We are, after all, at leisure."

"I won't be entirely at leisure," Jake said. "I'll be looking for opportunities."

"Maybe you can give Jake some advice." Vivian said. "About his painting, that is."

"I would be glad to." The widow smiled. "Shall we discuss it tonight at cocktails?"

"I always feel cocktails spoil one's dinner," Larissa said with a sniff.

"The cocktail hour is an essential part of life at the Waxwoodian, Larissa," said Marvina. "The courtyard gives a lovely view of the sea. Do come." With a gleam in her eye, she added, "It's the custom to ask others to join you at these resorts. You want to know the best people, don't you?"

His mother said with reluctance. "I suppose we shall have to go, then."

"I would appreciate all the help you can give me, Marvina." Jake tried to compensate for his mother's coldness.

The widow patted his arm. "It's nice to be needed by the younger generation."

The Griffiths, the second most influential family on Washington Street, now joined them. Mrs. Griffith came in first, a stately woman with eyes set too close together. Mr. Griffith followed meekly, a small man whose bushy beard tried to make up for his lack of stature. Huey, their son sported the same eyes as his mother, and Amber, their daughter, came in last, her skin sallow and her hair dull. She had recently married, but the husband, a staunch young man, was conspicuously absent from the party.

Larissa's eyes were alert as the Griffiths arranged themselves next to the Alderdices. Amber looked haughtily down at her hands folded neatly in her lap, waiting for instructions from her mother. Mr. Griffith immediately took on an air of masculine importance, leaving the social conversation to the women, soon absorbed in his newspaper.

Huey's emphatic eyes were immediately on Jake. "So now you can get on with it, eh?"

Jake looked at him with an even gaze as the train began to move. As a child, Huey had bullied younger boys in the neighborhood, and Jake had been one of his targets. Now twenty-eight, he had not lost that pugnacious leer.

"That's a crass way of putting it, don't you think?" Jake asked.

The man sniffed and unfolded his newspaper. While glancing at the headline, Huey asked, "What do you intend to do now?"

"Enjoy the summer, like yourself."

"I mean with your life," said the man. "It's time you decided, you know."

"So everyone keeps reminding me."

"Perhaps you need reminding," said Huey. "As I recall, you've hardly set foot in the Alderdice Shipping offices."

Jake glared at him. "I've had other pursuits."

The man looked up from the newspaper. "Such as?"

"Artistic pursuits."

"Oh, that." Huey went back to his reading. "I thought that was just a whim of your grandmother's."

Jake felt rage rising in his throat. "I would be obliged if you would speak respectfully about my grandmother."

Like all bullies, he shrank back at the challenge. "My apologies. But surely you don't mean what you say?"

"Why not?"

"Why, it would be foolish," Huey said. "Your grandfather built a damn good company, and you ought not to sniff at it."

"I've never sniffed at it," Jake insisted.

Huey looked down his nose. "I only meant, it's a logical conclusion you should take over after your grandfather's death. That's the way of things."

Jake mumbled, "Sometimes things aren't always the way people think they ought to be."

Huey folded his paper back in his lap and leaned forward. "I'm willing to bet money you have a head for it. It's only confidence you lack."

"I don't wish to discuss it further, Huey." Jake turned away from the man.

"Confidence is the thing," The man went on. "A man must build it up. Now, if you would take an interest in boxing, say, or wrestling or football—"

"My grandfather always thought those sports rather brutal," Jake interrupted.

"He would, I daresay," said Huey. "None of the older generation has really taken to it. I had a time persuading my father to attend our football games, but he's an enthusiast now. Aren't you, Father?" He glanced at the partridge-like man.

"Athletic prowess attests to a man's accomplishments elsewhere," Mr. Griffith mumbled.

"We've a team at the Hercules' Club," Huey continued. "I'll be leaving in a week, in fact, for summer training. If you joined us—"

"I've never played a game of football in my life," Jake said.

"It would do you a world of good."

"Make me heartier and more aggressive?" Jake grimaced. "Is that your idea of a man's place in the world?"

"It was your grandfather's idea.." A small pout appearing on Huey's lips as he unfolded his newspaper again.

"We all have our place in the world, Huey," Jake said. "One need not be better than the other."

"Mr. Roosevelt doesn't think so," said Huey. "He makes no secret of his fondness for sports."

Mr. Griffith suddenly slapped his knees and declared, "Young men are too pampered these days, we shall all go to the devil when the new century arrives." He eyed Jake with the red look of a bull. "How old are you, boy?"

Jake answered almost sheepishly, "Twenty-one."

"Huey, stop goading the boy." He gave his son a rueful look. "Not too late, not too late at all."

They were both looking at him now, their eyes popping and lips gaping, measuring him as a tailor measured a suit of clothes.

Jake rose. "One may be as studiousness about art as business."

"Bah!" The man picked up his paper again.

Jake glanced at his mother, suddenly anxious she might have heard the conversation and withdraw her support of his decision to become an artist. But she was absorbed in something Mrs. Griffith was saying, her hand on her chin, her face lit up with the hostess look he knew so well.

"If you'll excuse me, I think I'll get some air." Neither man seemed to notice as he headed for the doorway that led out to the connecting car.

CHAPTER 3

J ake hardly knew where to turn. He could still smell Huey's floral cologne. Huey, with his long neck and popping eyes, his insidious remarks and overblown pride. How he had looked at him just now as if he had a right to judge!

The wind swept away the smoke and untidied his hair, as he had forgotten his hat. He could see white sands and a whisk of green here and there as the train sped ahead. The movement of the train calmed him. He had no real resentment toward Huey or his father. Their narrow vision merely reflected the way others would judge him. These others , the patriarchs of Ancestor Hall, existed in painted eyes and broadly stroked faces, but they were no less real.

He remembered the day his grandfather had introduced him to the ancestors. The sunlight had filtered through the lace curtains at breakfast, and the maple syrup smelled sweet as he poured over his pancakes. His grandfather had been unusually silent the entire meal. He finished his coffee and dabbed the corners of his mouth with a linen napkin, as he always did. Then he looked at Jake with an anxious, tender gaze Jake had never seen before. The look lasted only a moment and Grandfather was once again his crisp-mannered self, but it was a look Jake would never forget.

Grandmother suggested Carlos, the gardener, help them lean a ladder against the oak tree so they could climb up and see the bird's nest she had discovered that morning. Grandfather answered in a resolute voice, "Jacob will come with me." Grandmother bowed her head in supposition, as she always did to Grandfather's wishes.

His grandfather swept him out of the dining room. Jake was frightened, but the man pressed his shoulder. "Don't worry, my boy. We're going to another part of the house." Jake's apprehension increased as he followed Grandfather. The man's steps were filled with the power and meaning of one who never wasted a moment, the walking stick he always carried digging into the ground.

It was the first time Jake realized how large Alderdice Hall was. They crossed the entire house. Rugs turned into wooden panels as they entered the East Wing. The double doors usually kept closed were open as if expecting them. The wooden panels turned to marble, and Grandfather picked up speed. Breathless but too terrified to say a word, Jake tried to keep up as best he could. Grandfather stopped and peered down at him . "Perhaps we're wrong. Perhaps it's too soon. You're just a child, really."

Jake swallowed, his throat feeling dry. "I'll be ten in a few months, Grandfather."

"A child," he repeated. "But so was I." This seemed to restore his resolve.

They reached a pair of maple doors. Grandfather took a large key out of his pocket, handling it gently as if it could crumble from age, and unlocked them. All Jake could see at first was another hallway that seemed to go on for eternity. Then his grandfather lit the gas lamps, and he saw the rows of picture frames.

He knew they were in Ancestor Hall even before Grandfather told him. He had heard the maids speaking of such a place in the house. Vivian vowed she would go there one day and see what it was all about. But as far as he knew, she never had.

That day, Jake heard stories about the men in the pictures, his grandfather's voice echoing toward the arched ceiling.

"This is your great-grandfather, Merton Carlyle," said Grandfather. "Learn from him, my boy. Anything but effort dulls a man's dignity." His mouth set hard. "He and I never had much regard for the fops of this world. Frivolous frolicking and that sort."

Jake peered up at his great-grandfather staring distractedly into the distance. He recalled Grandmother saying her father became "like an English lord" once Grandfather retired him and changed the name of Carlyle Shipping to Alderdice Shipping.

"Do you know why your grandfather let me take over the business?"

"Because you married Grandmother," Jake said.

Lightening entered Grandfather's blue eyes. "Because he knew I would never squander my pennies like the so-called sons of his wealthy friends. He knew I would take every cent I earned and put it back into the business."

"And did you, Grandfather?"

"My boy, I turned that small company into an empire. I made the Alderdice name mean something in this city."

The next portrait was Great-Uncle Floyd. The anemic-looking man gazed into space with his hands clasped at his chest. Grandfather mumbled something about the clergy, a monastery, and a defeat of Spanish conquistadors in the early days of California. That ended the story of Great-Uncle Floyd.

Several relatives whose names Jake could not recall followed. All were men, all bearded, and all smiling victoriously. How quickly he had forgotten those tall tales! He closed his eyes and tried to hear Grandfather's waspish voice over the roar of the train. *Army colonel, court judge, steel mill baron.*

They both stood silent when they reached the end of the hallway. Suddenly his grandfather said, "When you're a man, my boy, remember they'll be watching you. They'll be judging."

"Watching and judging?" Jake asked.

"You'll make your place in the world as they did," he said. "You'll add honor to the family name and not waste your life in idleness."

"I won't be a fiddler with life," Jake said, proud that he had adopted the phrase Grandfather was so fond of.

This made his grandfather smile. It wasn't the usual tight smile of a man who had no time for anything except business but a smile of genuine pleasure and understanding. "I once spent a summer with such men." Grandfather took his hand, leading him out of Ancestor Hall. "They thought life was a game, but it is not a game, my boy."

By the time they reached the main part of the house, Jake's terror had deteriorated. Despite his grandfather's warning, these ancestors were watching over him. He was comforted by these painted faces.

Jake stared through the dirty window of the parlor car door, seeing outlines of the Griffiths inside.

From that day, his grandfather took hold of his education. Jake no longer went with Vivian and the governess to the playroom. His grandfather hired tutors, stern taskmasters who admired and feared him enough to insure Jake had a proper course of study. Every evening after dinner, when they assembled in the upstairs parlor, Grandfather seated Jake in front of him and asked for an account of what he had learned that day. He listened, never interrupting or yawning with boredom. It was as if he enjoyed the knowledge Jake received, though he must have known Jake wouldn't remember much of what he had learned.

Grandfather had had little formal education and learned much of his elegant and didactic speech from books.

Jake sighed into the wind. The last time he had been in Ancestor Hall was two years ago when Grandfather's painting joined the majestic company. The portrait of Grandfather sitting behind his desk in his office at Alderdice Shipping was one neither he nor Vivian had ever seen. Rather than the usual austere gaze, his countenance was wry, even faintly amused. In that relaxed state, the handsomeness of his youth returned, lingering with the dignity of middle age.

Their mother had beamed and explained, "Your grandfather's loyal employees commissioned Stebbins to paint it."

"A noble gift," Jake murmured.

"Yes, it was," his mother agreed.

Vivian had glared up at it. "Every false memory is noble."

Later, Jake slipped back into the marble room alone and studied the portrait for a while. It hadn't occurred to Jake that he had anything to fear. Now with the train rattling under his feet and the wind slapping his chest, he was afraid. He realized now what Grandfather meant when he said the ancestors were watching him and judging. He would have to face trial in the afterlife with a jury of those skeletal ancestors. Would it be a fast trial, persecuting him for the life he would choose for himself, tearing through him like a beast ripping through the skin of its prey? Or would they bow their heads and say, "He has contributed to the family honor, let him be"?

CHAPTER 4

Chapter 4

The shaking train made him feel ill as he grasped the railing. He turned to go back into the parlor car, but caught sight of his mother. He was breathless again, and turned around. He slid open the door to the attached car and stepped inside.

He smelled the heady scent of mint and tobacco immediately. Only men were about. He realized he had entered the smoking car. A few elderly men sat solitary with a cigar and face buried behind a newspaper. A group of young men, all in blue jackets with matching pins on their lapels gathered in the corner. Although it was still morning, they were passing a bottle of whiskey between them. Each time a man poured himself a glass, they shouted out an enthusiastic toast to his health. The man tending the bar was polishing glasses, clearly disapproving of the scene. His head remained bent on his work, but his eyes raised with the narrow gaze of contempt. The elderly men either pretended not to notice the boys or were genuinely oblivious to their boisterous behavior.

The last occupant in the car was a man who sat near the door. His long legs stretched across the aisle, and he wide shoulder and torso filling the seat. Jake found him immediately imposing, his dark red hair groomed and his eyes a brilliant coal shade. He leaned a little to one side with an offhand gaze at the young men, though he seemed not to see them.

Jake cleared his throat, and the man immediately drew back his legs. Jake surveyed the rest of the car. The only other vacant seat was next to the redheaded man who studied him with a bald stare. He remembered Huey's judging eyes and studied the man openly and without remorse. The redhead's clothes were as immaculate as his clean-shaven face, and yet there was a sense of fumbling in the way the watch chain hung in the vest, the worn leather patches on the elbows, and the slightly askew bowtie peeking out from under the shirt collar.

The redhead leaned forward and put out his hand. "My name is Stevens."

Jake introduced himself and accepted the gesture. The man's shake was firm but lighter than he would have expected. "Stevens what?"

"Just Stevens." The man smiled. "Alderdice, did you say?" Jake nodded. "I recall seeing your picture in the paper a few years ago."

Jake remembered the drawing in the *Alta California* of the family standing near Grandfather's grave.

Stevens said in an appropriately hushed tone, "May I express my condolences for your loss?"

Jake glanced at the college boys. They turned toward the older man as if he were one of their lecturers. "Thank you." Jake could almost see his grandfather projected onto the window, his blue eyes replaced by gold, indistinguishable from a scarecrow, except for the lion-head cane he carried in the bony hand.

"My father met Malcolm Alderdice several times." Stevens' voice was mild and reassuring. "At the races, I believe."

"Your father?" Jake could not help noticing the man looked about Larissa's age.

The man smiled. "Your grandfather liked the races, yes?"

"He didn't go very often," Jake said. "He was too busy with his business."

"*His* business?" Stevens arched a brow.

Jake looked down at his hands. "I meant the family business."

The redhead leaned back. "You, however, have other plans." He reached for the cigar box on the table.

Jake eyed the man. "Are you a mind reader, Mr. Stevens?"

This caused a flurry among the college boys. Without turning to look at them, Stevens asked, "Roger, am I a mind reader?"

A young men with wary eyes answered, "I wouldn't be surprised, Harland." The others chuckled.

"My cousin, Roger Howe." Mr. Howe mumbled a greeting.

"Why don't you introduce Jake to your friends?" Stevens asked. "He looks about your age."

"Why don't *you*?" the young man shot back.

The redhead chuckled. "Because they're your friends."

Jake received handshakes from the five young men. He declined the drink Mr. McDonaugh offered him. One of the elderly men growled and shook his paper. Stevens uttered an apology.

"Men need the company of men." Stevens smiled. "I noticed you at the station with two ladies." He glanced at the college boys to see if they were absorbing his words. "The fair sex can be quite trying no matter how charming they are."

"One is my mother," Jake remarked.

The young men were amused, but Stevens silenced them with a glare. "Mothers are perhaps the most complex beings on earth." His dark eyes grew almost transparent. "Yes, complex beings."

Jake was becoming mesmerized by this man's quiet voice and imposing figure, staring glass-eyed out the window, though it was clear he was not interested in the scenery. A breath of smoke came his way from a heavy cigar lit by one of the college-aged men, and Jake coughed, covering his nose with his handkerchief.

"Fathers are more transparent," Stevens said.

"I wouldn't know about that," Jake mumbled.

"Oh?" The man was immediately alert.

"My father died when I was very young," said Jake. "My grandfather was the only father I had, really."

"A man does not let go of a father so easily," said the redhead with sympathy. "Whoever he may be."

Mr. Howe dropped his glass on the floor. It did not break, but rolled toward the wall. The elderly man who had grunted at them left the car, glaring back at the youth as if they were lice.

"A shame about your father." The redhead looked at him. "How old are you?"

"Twenty-one."

"You're just at a time of life when a father becomes a young man's necessary guide."

"I've gotten along without one for the last several years," Jake said. "I expect I won't suffer too much without one now."

"You never can tell, friend." The ray of sunlight from the window made Stevens' eyes glitter. "I am at your disposal if you need any advice."

Jake met Mr. Howe's gaze. The young man set his glass down on the counter, and the bartender snatched it up, wiping it clean.

"Roger will be of age in another few years." The redhead nodded toward him. "Ah, I don't envy the lot of you."

"Why do you say that?"

"There are too many ways a young man can abandon his mind these days," the redhead mused. "When I was your age, we hadn't as many ways to lose our heads." He chuckled.

"I suppose that's true," Jake agreed.

"We had our pleasures, of course. But we took them after we established ourselves in the world."

"You have no hope for us, then?" Jake couldn't help but smile.

"On the contrary." The man returned the smile. "I have great faith in youth." He leaned forward, showing a trace of freckles on his uneven skin. "What are these plans of yours, the ones you prefer over the family business?"

"I'm a painter." Jake heard a scoff escape from the sea of blue jackets and thought it sounded like Mr. Howe. "I intend to be an artist."

"Admirable." The redhead sounded sincere. "Few young men would have the courage to make such a bold move." He crossed his legs. "Especially a young man with other prospects such as yourself."

"Prospects?"

"Your family business, of course." Stevens studied Jake. "I'm no authority on art, but I may say I'm as passionate about it as I am about hunting and fishing."

"Admirable," Jake said.

"I spent time with painters in Europe," the redhead continued. "Some of them quite revolutionary. Have you heard of Symbolism?"

"Only vaguely." He could feel the college boys squinting at him.

"You've talent, I'm sure."

"I was told I had."

"Told?" Stevens threw his head back and laughed. His laugh was deep befitting a man his size. One elderly men dropped his newspaper and stared at Stevens. The redhead smiled and bowed.

"If you intend to become a painter," he remarked, "you ought to be more assured about it."

Jake shrugged. "I've had four years of training from one of the most prominent art teachers in San Francisco. He told me my work would speak for itself."

Stevens put his hands together. "A rather old-fashioned notion, I'm afraid. My father's generation was the generation of a man of his word. These days, one must do everything possible to make one's word the loudest."

The college boys had even stopped their drinking game and were listening with attention, their eyes staring with fascination.

"Someone else has been trying to convince me a man may have confidence only when he has mastered the art of competition," Jake said, thinking of Huey.

Stevens laughed again, filling the entire car with the pleasant roar. "Perhaps he's right." He leaned back, folding his hands behind his head. "'We need prowess, and there is no reason we should not have it. But a man needs character more than prowess.'"

"Amply put, Mr. Roosevelt." A young man introduced to Jake as Mr. Trent said with a bow. Chuckles escaped the group, earning a snarl from the elderly man still wrapped up in his paper.

"What sort of paintings do you do?" Stevens asked. "What subject, I mean?"

"Landscape," he answered.

"You'll find plenty of inspiration in Waxwood," Stevens assured him. "You've read about the wax wood forest, I'm sure."

"I'm told they're an anomaly," said Jake. "I'm eager to see them for myself."

"Take the path to the hill that leads in from the beach," the man advised. "Not the main road. You'll reach the heart of the woods that way." He cocked his head. "You're staying at The Waxwoodian?"

"Yes."

"Fine place," said Stevens. "Bit of an enormity, as far as hotels go. We shall see something of one another, then."

"I hope so, sir," Jake said.

"And will we see an exhibit of your paintings at one of the galleries?" the redhead asked.

"I'm not sure," said Jake. "I'm still exploring the best avenues."

"Perhaps I might assist you there."

"That's awfully kind of you, Mr. Stevens." Jake had doubts

whether the man was doing more than trying to make an impression with his assured tone and set shoulders.

"Call me Stevens, I said."

"Stevens," Jake mumbled.

"Character. Not like the others, no," Jake heard him murmur. He lingered for a moment, thinking he might say something more. But the man was lost in thought.

CHAPTER 5

They reached Waxwood in the late afternoon. The place seemed hardly more than the sort of coastal town men boasted of retreating to with their lady friends that Jake had heard about. Distant hills revealed strange trees he guessed were the infamous wax woods. People strolled the pier and fishermen cast their lines, squinting into the sun.

Vivian sighed. "It hasn't changed much at all."

"No," he said softly, thinking with distate at the trip he had taken with Vivian when he was only fifteen. "It hasn't."

"Just wait," Marvina said with a knowing look.

"How do we reach the hotel?" Larissa inquired in the general direction of the Griffiths.

Huey answered her with an air of authority, "We take a boat across."

"Boat? Oh, dear." Larissa glanced at the luggage piled on to the cart.

Mrs. Griffith smiled. "Don't worry, my dear. The boats are almost as big as our yacht in the city."

"Why must we take a boat?" Vivian asked.

"The hotels are on the other side of the bay," Marvina said. "It's a bustling little town."

"I don't know if I would call it 'bustling.'" Jake glanced at the signs and shops behind them. "It looks rather deserted, in fact."

"Not compared to what it was," the widow mused. "Now I shall have to say, 'there is everything here.' Everything people like us would want."

He looked down the wooden path. The bay looked scant compared to the one in San Francisco, and the trees he had seen gave an odd discomfort to this tranquil setting.

"There was a half-submerged boathouse there." Vivian nodded at the second pier. "I rather admired its endurance."

"They've replaced it with houseboats." Jake stared at the row of white boats gleaming in the sun.

Larissa smiled. "Now you see why I told you there would be no ghosts this time."

Vivian stiffened. "Specters don't disappear so easily, Mother."

This remark made Amber Griffith cast a ruffled eye. "Ghosts and burials! My, Vivian, you have a morbid imagination."

His sister gave her a sweet smile. "A little ghost and grave adds interest to one's life."

The young woman gave Vivian a fearful look and ambled to her mother's side. Jake felt his sister had infected him with her nervousness. The back of his neck felt damp.

They found the boat waiting for them which, as Mrs. Griffith had promised, had ample space for passengers and baggage. As Jake stood on deck, he saw Stevens and the young men trudging down the main road toward the pier, their eyes avoiding in the glare of the heavy sun.

The boat made its way across the water in the general direction of the bridge. Jake wondered where the bay would merge with the sea. A stretch of sand greeted their arrival, framed by a long boardwalk already well worn by the treading of slippers and boots. Hotels and inns dominated its edge. One appeared to Jake as overly lavish and ornate, a labyrinth of towers, roofs, and verandas. The embossed sign of *The Waxwoodian* stretched above the entrance in gold letters.

"This is all part of Waxwood now?" Vivian asked.

"Shrewd businessmen realized the gold mine lying in wait here about five years ago," Marvina answered. "A rather pleasant little place, isn't it?"

"And peaceful," Jake pointed out. "One can see that."

"Peaceful only because it's isolated from the rest of the town," Vivian remarked.

"I rather think that adds to its dignity." Larissa smiled.

his sister glanced at her. "You always were one for exclusivity, weren't you, Mother?"

"No, dear," Larissa answered. "Only privacy."

"My suffragist friends say there's quite a bit of activity in the old section of town," Marvina said. "Of their sort, that is."

"Oh?" Vivian perked up.

"I hope you won't involve yourself with *them* while you're here, Mrs. Moore," Larissa said. "Not a very amicable way of spending one's vacation."

"In other words, Mother will snub you if you do," Vivian said.

Marvina seemed amused. "I wouldn't blame you if you did, Larissa. Summer leisure is not the time for politics. I've been told one of them is going to organize a sort of library for working women one day. That I should like to see."

"I wouldn't think working women had the time nor the inclination for reading," said Larissa dryly.

"All women have a right to education now, Mother," said Vivian. "Some of us even enjoy reading." Larissa flashed her a look.

They were herded through revolving glass doors trimmed with heavy gold emblems of the hotel name. The lobby was rich yellow and white with pictures etched in gold frames, a stark contrast to the warmer burgundy and olive furniture. The high ceiling curved into a mural of a forest with twinkling fairies and a woman beautifully wrapped in tulle with delicate features. "Titania and her followers?" Jake suggested.

"In the wax wood forest, no less," Marvina said. "I recognize the trees. Rather clever."

"We won't keep you, Mrs. Moore," Larissa said briskly. "If you would rather go ahead of us, I'm sure they'll assign you a room very quickly."

Marvina took the hint and motioned to a bellboy. "I'll see you all later for cocktails." She pressed Vivian's hand and winked at Jake.

His mother glared at his sister. "I don't intend for you to spend much time with that woman, dear."

"I won't spend all my time with her," Vivian promised.

"You won't spend *any* time with her, if I can help it." Larissa lowered her voice. "There are many opportunities in a place such as this for an intelligent and charming young woman. And your brother can make some wonderful connections for himself."

"You make us sound like politicians." Vivian grimaced. "Whose votes would you like us to win, Mother? Theirs? Or hers? Or his?" As she spoke, she pointed her parasol at random people, most of whom were elderly and looked lost in the chattering crowd. Jake laughed.

"I don't ask for miracles, dear," Larissa said in a dry voice. "Only a little cooperation from both of you."

"May I assume you shall not expect me to speak to anyone over the age of thirty, then?" Vivian asked, amused. "Or is it forty?"

"A lady may make an advantageous marriage to a man of advanced years." Jake was quoting what he had heard his mother and other Washington Street matrons say at parties and balls.

"Like my father was advantageous?" Vivian's eyes sparkled. "Mother said he was fourteen years her senior."

"Thirteen," Larissa corrected.

"A man is hardly an advantage to a lady when he dies of heart failure after only eight months of marriage," Jake murmured.

"That is a horrible thing to say about your sister's father!" Larissa snapped.

"You can't deny some women are quite content to marry gents they know won't last until the silver anniversary," Vivian said.

"The freedom of having been married without really having to be married," Jake added.

"You're both behaving very crudely," Larissa said. But the lightness in her tone confirmed what he and Vivian had realized long ago: Her two husbands had been a necessary evil rather than a wish fulfilled.

The crowd had dispersed, and just as the bellboy motioned them toward the reception desk, the boisterous voices of Mr. Howe and his friends rose behind them. Their drinking game had left them quite intoxicated, and some of the young men were walking a little unsteadily. Despite the prominent *No smoking permitted in the lobby* sign, vile smoke from the young men's cigars filled the air . People glared and held their handkerchiefs to their noses, but the young men hardly noticed or cared.

A middle-aged man in a uniform approached the group as they reached an empty window, ousting a middle-aged couple, who backed away in horror. "Now, look here! " The man shook a finger at them. "You've got to go to the end of the line!"

Mr. Howe slid a bill out of his coat pocket. "Won't you help us, sir?"

"Who's responsible for you lot?" The man sneered.

"I am." Stevens appeared from the crowd, towering above them, his broad shoulders accentuating his imposing frame. He was striking with his dark red hair and pale skin. People stared at him in awe.

"Their headmaster?" Vivian whispered.

"Let us hope, dear," Larissa answered.

"Harland Stevens, at your service." The redhead bowed with natural ease and dignity.

"Mr. Stevens, if your friends cannot behave themselves, they shall have to leave," the man said.

"And you are?"

"Mr. Hughes, sir, the manager of this hotel."

"Pleased to meet you, Mr. Hughes." The redhead smiled pleasantly. "I will attend to the matter." His voice lowered to a growl directed at the young men. "Put out those cigars!"

A snort came from a pug belonging to a rather portly woman a slight distance away. The redhead reached down and petted the dog's head, engaging the woman in conversation about dogs that extracted a dimpled grin and shrill giggle.

"A rather odd papa for them," Vivian remarked.

"Not papa," Jake said. "Chaperone."

"A wise man not to make a scene," Larissa said with a nod.

Stevens motioned the college boys aside. His words were inaudible, but his mild voice vibrated across the lobby in a way that made Jake feel uneasy. Repentance replaced arrogance on the young men's faces. Although Mr. Howe's countenance remained defiant, he apologized to Mr. Hughes and the elderly couple he and his friends had expelled from the line and retreated to the back along with his friends.

Larissa's eyes shone with admiration. "This chaperone, as you call him, seems to have his charges well in hand."

"His name is Stevens." His mother and sister glanced at him. "I met him on the train."

"He might be a valuable man to know, Jacob," Larissa said.

"Who are all those young men with him?" Vivian asked.

"Mr. Howe, his cousin, and his cousin's school mates."

"Now you can see why your grandfather thought it best not to send you to college," Larissa remarked.

"I don't like him," Vivian declared.

"The cousin is a little trying," Jake agreed.

"I meant Mr. Stevens."

Their mother blinked. "You've no cause to say such a thing, dear. You don't even know the man."

"You don't have to know some people to get an impression of them," said his sister. "Mr. Stevens looks like the type who pierced dragonflies with a pin when he was a boy just to see what was in their transparent bodies."

"What a gruesome idea." Larissa wrinkled her face. "I'm sure Mr. Stevens is as decent and pleasant as he appears. Isn't he, Jacob?"

Jake watched Stevens lording over the college men, directing them like a heavenly father.

CHAPTER 6

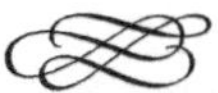

They settled into their suite with just enough time to dress for the cocktail hour which, according to the card the bellhop had given them, took place every evening at five o'clock. The courtyard looked like a heart-shaped meadow, each curve padding out just to the edge of the boardwalk. Small plots of flowers complemented the grass where gold-painted iron tables and chairs competed with the brightness of the sun. Tall hedges bordered the edge of the heart, high enough to hide guests from people strolling the boardwalk but still allowed them to gaze at the gaping blue sea.

"It's lovely here," Vivian breathed.

"Restful," Larissa agreed.

"I see now why this is a popular place," Jake said. "One may get one's bearings here." He breathed in the floral scent mixed with the sea.

"Bertha said Waxwood was a place where one may lose one's bearings," Vivian said softly.

"Did she?" His mother did not look at her.

"In her note to us," Vivian said. "You opened it with the

condolences for Grandmother, remember?" Her smile vanished gave him a burdened feeling.

Marvina appeared wearing a hat with a wide brim and a scarf around her slim neck. She waved at them, her face relaxed. "Heavenly place, isn't it?" she sat down next to Vivian.

"Jake thinks it's the proper place for rejuvenation," said Vivian.

"Heavens, you make it sound so melodramatic," said Marvina. "I always thought you were grave when you were a boy, Jake."

"I don't mean to be." He was a little stung by her words.

"You were always the somber one," Larissa agreed. "Your grandfather said you would grow out of it."

"Perhaps he would have if Grandfather hadn't impressed upon him the evils of leisure," said Vivian. "I shall never forget how he used to come into the playroom and shout 'Nothing to do, my boy? Don't idle, don't idle. We shall find you something meaningful!'"

Marvina laughed as she accepted a cocktail. "Your grandfather had some rather rigid ideas."

"Not rigid, Mrs. Moore," said Larissa in an icy tone. "Upstanding."

"He was rigid with Jake," Vivian said, "He didn't seem to care whether I squandered my hours away."

"There is no pity for a young man who wastes his time, but a young woman is allowed to whittle it away," the widow agreed. "All is forgiven, because the poor lamb probably hasn't anyone to tell her what to do nor the presence of mind to do it herself."

"Isn't that a rather dismal portrait of womanhood?" Jake raised an eyebrow.

"If you were a woman, you wouldn't say that," Vivian snapped. "You would know what Marvina means."

"Don't blame him for his ignorance, dearest." Marvina winked at her.

Larissa cleared her throat. "I don't intend to allow Vivian to whittle away her hours any more than I intend that Jake should idle away his."

The widow looked at her with her elongated eyes. "You seem to have definite plans for someone who's come to take a rest."

"Not *my* plans, Mrs. Moore," she said. "My children's."

"They are no longer children," Marvina reminded her.

"That is precisely my point," Larissa retorted.

"What Mother means," said Vivian, "is that she intends for me to find a new husband now that my mourning is over."

"Not the worst idea I've heard," Marvina remarked. "*If* you intend to marry again someday."

"Someday," said his sister. "But not now."

"Many happy unions originated in resorts such as this," Larissa insisted.

"Viv said she hasn't that notion in mind at the moment, Mother," Jake said. Larissa shot him a caustic look.

Marvina called the waiter to replenish her cocktail. "With so many opportunities open for young ladies nowadays, you think of that one! In the words of Albina Fowler, 'If a woman is to progress, let her progress be mental and not matrimonial.'"

"And who is Albina Fowler?"

"A friend of mine," said the widow. "An eloquent speaker and one of our leaders."

"She means the suffragists, Mother," Vivian added.

"Is it Mrs. or Miss?" Larissa asked archly.

"Several times Mrs.," Marvina said. "She thinks we all ought to progress, men and women both. Only women ought to do the speaking and men the listening for once."

"The ground under our feet is in constant motion even when we don't feel it," Vivian mused.

"You're becoming scientific, Vivian," his mother said.

"She isn't," said Jake. "Miles told us all about it."

"Even Mother Nature knows one can't stay in one place forever." There was a desperation in his sister's voice. "The world is always spinning. I'm sometimes frightened I shall fall into oblivion if I don't spin with it."

"So am I," Jake murmured.

"I don't think either of you need worry." Marvina patted Vivian's hand. "I know you'll make something of yourself, dearest. And as for you, Jake—" she looked at him with affection, "I shall help all I can."

"Thank you." He bowed.

"Allow me to congratulate you on your new endeavor."

"Endeavor?"

"You want to be an artist," said the widow. "That takes courage."

"Someone else on the train told me the same thing."

"What do you suggest, Marvina?" Vivian leaned forward.

"I can only speak from an outsider's the point of view, of course," she said.

"Jacob, I don't think—" his mother began.

"You said you expect Jake to fulfill his duty," Vivian insisted. "What harm could it do to ask for help in fulfilling it?"

"Mrs. Moore admits herself she is no expert."

"I'm still a knowledgeable outsider," Marvina insisted. "Jake asked me for advice, and I am ready to give it."

"Please do," Jake said.

"First, consider going to Europe," said the widow. "Find some master who studied or taught at one of the highly established arts schools. The Academié de Beaux Arts, for instance."

"Why must he go all the way to Paris?" asked Vivian. "Jake's had four years of study here."

"We've no real good art instruction here, not even in San Francisco," she said. "Most artists don't have the means to go abroad, but you do. It would put you at an enormous advantage, Jake."

"What about a patron?" asked Larissa.

Marvina laughed. "Gone are the days when kings and arch-bishops commissioned artists."

"Then how do they earn their living?"

"Through their own efforts, of course," said the widow. "Art is a business just like any other, and a respectable one at that. Mary Cassatt, for example—"

"A woman artist?" His mother's eyes narrowed with surprise.

"I told you, many opportunities are open to women these days outside of marriage," said Marvina. "Cassatt has been rather successful with her womanly portraits. I don't imagine Jake could do worse."

"We shall see how well Jacob does first," said Larissa.

"Perhaps you can show me some paintings you've brought with you," Marvina said.

"I've brought none with me."

The widow chuckled. "Your modesty will do you in, dearest. My artist friends have no qualms about pulling their sketchbooks out of their pockets at the least sign of interest. It's hard work selling yourself, they say."

"That has such a terrible ring to it." Vivian shuddered. "Almost like a harlot on the street."

"Vivian!"

"I agree it isn't a pleasant way of putting it," said the widow. "But if one is to be frank—"

"That's your trouble, Mrs. Moore," Larissa said. "Sometimes you're too frank."

"Too frank for a woman, Mother means," Vivian added.

Marvina wrapped her shawl closer around her shoulders. "We've been told so many lies in this century, let us hope we can be more truthful in the next."

"We're not in the new century *yet*," Larissa reminded her.

"It's coming, Larissa," said the widow. "Nobody can stop it, not even you and your kind, with your outworn ideas."

His mother gave a little sniff and looked to the sea.

"You've nothing to show anyone who asks you, then?" Marvina looked at Jake.

"I brought my paint box and some materials," he offered.

"Splendid," said the woman. "Then do a painting or two and show them to the galleries here. There are a good number of them past the boardwalk. Use as much local color and landscape as you can. That ought to impress them."

"I don't know as I like that idea," Larissa said.

"Why not, Mother?" Vivian glanced at her.

"It seems so undignified." His mother shifted away from the table.

"Like a harlot on the street?" the widow asked with a wary smile.

"I prefer you reframe from using such vulgar language in front of my children," Larissa snapped. "What you say to your own friends is your own business."

"Jake would know where he stands," Marvina pointed out.

His mother looked at the sea again without answering.

"You really think it will do any good?" Jake asked.

"Well, you must start *somewhere*, dearest." The widow leaned back. "You know, Larissa, you ought to be very proud of Jake. He is an uncommon young man, and that's saying much these days."

"After the little display we saw with those boys this afternoon, I should think so," Vivian agreed.

"Yes, they were rather horrendous, weren't they?" Marvina chuckled.

"Mr. Stevens took charge of them very well," Larissa insisted.

"Mr. Stevens?"

"The man with the red hair. Their chaperone, I'm told," said his mother.

"I believe he's educating them for the summer," Jake said. "I spoke with Mr. Stevens on the train."

"I can't imagine he'll have a very pleasant time of it."

"I wonder what his *real* reason is," Vivian murmured.

"What do you mean?" He glanced at his sister.

"The way he handled them this afternoon," she said. "He was watching them all along, you know, before he stepped in. Almost as if he were amused to see them behaving like savages."

"You imagined it, dear," said Larissa.

Jake couldn't help but think of how he had felt int he smoking car with Stevens' lecturing and observing.

A waiter struck a gong signaling the end of the cocktail hour. Women lifted their skirts off of sandy steps, and men bent down under the low archway, their stride lazy and elegant.

Larissa gathered her gloves and fan.

"Oh, Mother, let's sit here a while longer," Vivian pleaded.

"One must never be late for dinner." Her mother said. "It gives the wrong impression."

"I don't think anyone cares," Jake said.

"The right people care." She lifted her eyes. "Always keep that in mind."

Marvina laughed. "You ought to open a finishing school, Larissa."

"Mother is a fine one to lecture on social etiquette," Vivian agreed.

Larissa glared at the widow. "I shall never have to work and neither will my daughter."

"You have no qualms about sending Jake off to work," Vivian pointed out.

"That's quite different." Her mother rose. "Jake is a man."

"A man must find his place," Jake added. "Grandfather said so."

"I wonder what your grandfather's opinion was of women and their place," said Marvina.

"I should think that's obvious," said Vivian. "A woman's place is the cage in which her family and her husband place her."

"Grandfather never said that," Jake insisted.

"There are some things one needn't say," his sister retorted.

"You're wrong, dear." Larissa pursed her lip. "Your grandfather thought women ought to occupy their time."

"Yes, but with what?" Marvina's eyes were sly. "I don't suppose he approved much of our recent political occupations."

"No," said Larissa sharply. "He didn't."

"And you, Mother?" Vivian gave her an icy stare. "What do you think?"

"There is women's work, and there is women's work," said his mother. "Women's work for women like us is not *wage* work."

"Someday, I might want to work for wages just like Jake," said Vivian. "And I won't be ashamed of it either."

As they filed through the French glass doors, Jake caught the look on his mother's face. The lines were tight with the cold-hearted look he remembered so well from his grandfather during the last months of his life.

CHAPTER 7

The next morning, Jake slipped into the hallway with his painting materials while his mother and sister were still asleep. The sun itself was hardly awake, and he met very few people as he trudged down the boardwalk. He found the path that led up the hill, just as Stevens had described it on the train. Something about the flapping branches and unmarked bark of the wax wood trees filled him with anticipation. The deadness that had weighed him down after his grandfather's funeral lifted.

He stepped along the path looking about him, growing used to the compressed air of the close trees. He was only seven when he discovered his grandmother's drawing of a fish hidden behind a curtain her room. The fish stared at him with frightened eyes, a skeleton of a thing sketched with an unsteady hand. That night, he took paper and pencil and drew a tree he had seen that morning when the nanny took them out for a walk.

"What is that you have there, my boy?" Grandfather asked.

Reluctantly, Jake handed the drawing to his grandfather. He expected him to laugh or scold. He examined the tree for some time, then held it out to Grandmother. "This ought to please you, Penelope."

His grandmother's attention had been on the tune she was teaching Vivian at the piano. Her smile faded as she studied the drawing.

"Aren't you pleased, Grandmother?" he ventured.

She looked at him, and he was alarmed to see there were tears in her eyes.

His mother, as always, was more practical. "Where did you get the paper and pencil, Jacob?"

"From me," Grandmother blurted out. "I gave it to him."

He did not know why she lied, but Larissa only shrugged. "Well, if he has an interest in it, I suppose it couldn't hurt to find a tutor, could it, Father?"

"Boy ought to get a well-rounded education," Grandfather agreed. "I've no objection, if we can find someone respectable and not some bohemian."

"Mrs. Breen was telling me the other day about a man she engaged for Hannah who has some reputation—"

"There is no need," Grandmother interrupted. "I shall be his tutor."

His mother and grandfather stared at her. Grandfather spoke first, "Penelope, my dear, you haven't the time."

"I shall make the time," she insisted.

"Are you sure that's wise, Mother?" Larissa asked.

"Jake may develop a passion for it," said his grandmother. "Tutors don't have passion. They do the job they're paid for."

"But it's been so long since you've done —"

"I still remember how!" Grandmother's voice shook the room like the cry of a bird.

His mother appealed to Grandfather. Jake had seen that look between them many times, but this time there was a strange alarm in her eyes.

Grandfather, however, was resolute. "There can be no harm in it, no harm in it *now*."

His grandmother took him to the pier, then to Ocean Beach,

then to another side of the bay that even the seagulls had forgotten. She explained to him about the fine details, how to see what others were unwilling or had no interest in seeing. She guided his hand in the oval shapes of fishes, their staring eyes and layered gills. He drew them tolerably well for one so young. But he felt nothing toward them, no connection and no affection.

It was only when he persuaded her to take him to the woods that his imagination came to life. She had taken him to a place in the mountains of San Francisco where the redwoods clustered together. Among them, he had felt less afraid of a world, less tiny and lost. He was a giant among other giants, protected and warmed by their nearness in a way he was not in Alderdice Hall. He saw what Vivian had seen long before — the house Grandfather built for Grandmother whispered secrets, a veneer of respectability protecting the Unmentionables.

Jake reached a clearing with wax wood trees. Shafts of sunlight ran in between branches and leaves. The grass was soft like velvet on his hands, couching orange. violet and blue wildflowers. Tiny frogs and finger-length salamanders slithered about as birds flapped their wings, though he could not see them.

He set his easel down and painted the trees in the clearing, the drooping branches with the firm ones, the salamanders and yellow centers of the flowers. He was back in that place of childhood with his grandmother's quiet but consolatory presence where nothing cruel or demanding could touch him.

A bush crumpled behind him. His startled gaze met Stevens' dark eyes as the man emerged from the parting of trees, giving him an amiable tip of his hat. "Sorry to disturb you."

"You're not." Jake felt his throat tighten as he tried to hide the painting.

Stevens grinned. "Nothing like taking an early morning walk in these woods."

"How did you happen to come here?"

"You sound suspicious, friend."

"I've been told the wax woods aren't exactly a favorite of visitors."

"They're a favorite of mine," said the redhead. "I've been in Waxwood once before, and they always fascinated me."

"But why this particular spot?"

The man laughed, leaning against a tree. "You're right, of course. I didn't just happen to come here. You made me curious."

"I did?"

"I'm a restless sleeper, especially in the summer," said Stevens. "I'm usually up before dawn. I have a suite on the same side as yours."

"You saw me leave the hotel." Jake guessed.

"You looked very determined."

Jake couldn't help but smile. "That made you curious?"

"I knew where you were going," said the man. "You told me you were a painter, after all."

"So you came to see if the wax woods would inspire me just as you promised?" Jake eyed him.

"I'm cursed with an intensely inquisitive nature," the redhead admitted.

"You and my sister have something in common," Jake smiled.

Stevens laughed. "A woman once told me I have the unpleasant habit of walking into other people's private moments."

"Maybe she was right." Jake thought of their conversation on the train.

"Women have a nasty talent for ferreting out a man's vulnerabilities, don't they?" The man glanced around. "I must confess, though, this is the first time I've seen these trees up close."

"Rather extraordinary, aren't they?"

"Trees are trees, friend." He rose. "Until some artist comes along and makes something extraordinary of them. May I?"

Jake hesitated, as he had never shown his paintings to anyone but his sister.

"I'm an observer," the redhead reminded him. "Not an art critic."

Stevens studied the painting, then turned to him with a satisfied smile. "I see what you meant when you said your grandmother taught you to see the fine details."

"You like it, then?" Jake held his breath.

"Very much," said the redhead. "I always thought too many American artists seem intent on capturing exactly what they see in front of them. I suppose that's what they call realism."

"You don't like that?"

"I told you I visited the Symbolist painters a few years ago," said Stevens. "They use religion and mythology to go deeper than what they see."

"Yes, I've read about that," said Jake.

"May I make a suggestion, purely from an observer's point of view?"

Jake's stomach tightened. "Please do."

"Something is missing."

Jake looked down at the net of fallen leaves. "I've felt that for some time."

"It's fine work." Stevens was instantly reassuring. "But it needs something more alive."

"A few more wood creatures maybe?"

"No, no." The man paced with one hand on his hip. A salamander slithered out of sight. Stevens watched the creature disappear. "Something magical."

"I don't—"

"A woman, I'd say." He stared at the painting. "Not a woman you would see walking down the street, but one who is ethereal."

"Yes," he said. "Yes, I see what you mean."

Stevens became thoughtful for a moment. "Your sister sat next to you last night at dinner, didn't she?"

"Vivian, yes," said Jake.

"She would be the perfect model for your wood scene."

Jake stared at him. "You mean I ought to ask her to pose for me?"

"Why not?" The redhead's eyes glittered in the sun. "I can see her as a nymph or huntress in the middle of this splendid wilderness."

Jake gazed at the painting. He thought of a statue of Diana, her marble figure erect, one hand grasping an arrow while the other rested on the head of a deer. He remembered the determined look on the goddess' face, ready to forge ahead.

"I'll do as you say, Stevens," he murmured.

The man waved at him as he brushed away the few leaves that had fallen on his square shoulders. "I'll leave you to your work." He disappeared among the trees.

Jake tried to work but his concentration waned so he gathered his materials and walked back to the hotel, his mind befuddled. When he entered the courtyard, the college boys were gathered on the grass. He nodded as he passed but did not speak. Most of them did likewise. Only Mr. Howe watched him with smoldering eyes.

CHAPTER 8

$\mathcal{J}$ake knew he would have a hard time persuading Vivian to pose for him. When their cousin Beatrice bought a Pocket Kodak and wanted to snap photos of Vivian, his sister refused, insisting she would not have people gaping at her like a prize cow. He timed his actions very carefully at breakfast the next day.

"Viv, how about coming to look at the wax woods with me?"

"Yes, why don't you, dear?" his mother murmured, half absorbed in the mail she had picked up from the desk. "You enjoy a good, brisk walk."

"I went painting there yesterday," he said, encouraged by Larissa's approval. "I think Vivian would like it there."

"I've been there," said his sister quietly. "It's a strange place, not quite — sane."

"Surely you exaggerate, Vivian." His mother gave her a look.

"Perhaps I do, a little," she admitted, breaking a slice of toast in two.

"I'd love the company." His hands dampen.

"Mrs. Tisher is organizing a boat race for the young people," his mother remarked. "Just be sure to be back in time."

"You know I don't care for boats," he said.

"Fern will be very disappointed," she insisted.

"Mother, she's barely eighteen!"

Vivian's eyes sparkled. "How anxious you are lately to trap us both into matrimony!"

His mother returned her sarcasm with a grim smile. "You're making more of it than there is, as usual. I only wish to see both of you settled in life."

Their eyes locked for a moment. Then, his sister speared a strawberry. "All right, dear. I'll go with you. And if we aren't back in time, I suppose Fern Tisher and Mr. Enoch Dumble will have to get along without us."

The grim smile returned on Larissa's face as she tore open another envelope.

People were emerging from breakfast when they set out. They watched as children with their sand pails and shovels, older people under enormous hats, and bathers in their skirted bathing suits flocked toward the floating waters. "It's much calmer here than at Ocean Beach," Vivian remarked.

"I always found Ocean Beach disquieting," he admitted.

"You're rather disquieted yourself, Jake."

"If you were a man, you would understand," he said.

"Don't think we women don't have our own troubles!"

He laughed and tossed a handful of sand at her as she darted away.

He was surprised to see Vivian knew the path into the forest. Her steps moved with assurance. "*Dans le fond des forêts votre image me suit.* Miss Gilbert read Racine to me in the playroom while you were with your tutors, and I remember that line."

"What made you think of it now?" he asked.

Vivian eased her hat down over her eyes. "You remember that French cousin of the Marsdens who came to visit last summer? I asked him what it meant. He said it was something like, 'Through the forest, your image follows me.'"

"You're too reliant on ghosts, Viv." But he felt himself the shadow of his grandmother, breathing warm against his cheek.

They reached the wax wood trees, but these differed from the place he had discovered the day before. Here, they were more serene but also more ominous, their shades darker, and the wood creatures around them more cautious. It seemed just the place where Diana would rest.

He blurted out, "Pose for me, Viv." She stared at him. "I'm tired of landscape," he stuttered. "Stevens thinks my paintings are missing a human element."

"Does he?" she asked sharply. "He knows nothing about how you paint."

"He knows enough about painting," Jake insisted. "He has artist friends in Europe."

"Did Mr. Stevens suggest you make me the human element in your work?"

"He thought you would make a splendid Diana," he admitted.

"You mean he wants you to make me an absurd object of play!"

"You don't give me much credit as an artist, Viv." He tried to sound light.

"I'm not eager to be immortalized in oils and cloth in the guise of a Roman goddess,," she snarled. "I'm sure Mr. Stevens thought I would find it flattering."

"Please, Viv," he pleaded. "I'm asking you, not him."

The indignation on her face evaporated. "It's really that important to you, dear?" He nodded. His sister smiled and kissed his cheek.

Jake was anxious as he arranged her against the background. She looked strikingly innocent that morning in her white dress with shiny red-blond hair. He first leaned her up against a wax wood tree but that seemed too much like a portraiture. Then he placed her sitting on a rock, but she looked like a puppet waiting for her master to bring her to life. He suddenly thought about the paintings he had seen in a gallery window in San Francisco of fairies in the woods, the tiny, illuminated creatures in flowing garments lying between blades of grass. He arranged her on her side with her head resting on her arm amidst beds of wild mushrooms and clover. The wax wood trees sheltered her with elongated leaves stretched like cat's tails.

He became so engrossed in painting, the figure of the fairy among the wild mushrooms and spiked leaves forming so perfectly to the picture in his mind that he was startled when is sister's voice rose with alarm. "We're not alone!"

He glanced around and discovered the towering figure through the trees. "Good morning, Stevens."

Vivian sat up, smoothing down her skirt. "I resent this intrusion, Mr. Stevens."

"I beg your pardon, Miss Alderdice." Jake detected a note of amusement in his voice. "One never knows what one might find walking in these woods."

"My sister thinks it's like hell here," Jake mused.

"I never said that!"

"Insane, then," Jake countered. "You said *that*, didn't you, Viv?"

"I agree." The redhead retrieved a stick lying on the ground. "Fascinating as they are, no one can look at these trees and think them anything but Luna's creation." He tapped the slippery bark so it gave way, making an imprint.

"They are real, Mr. Stevens," said Vivian.

"As real as the wind makes a devil's nest of a pretty woman's mane."

Her hands flew to her hair. She had removed her hat, and the wind pulled strands apart from the coiled braid.

"It's impertinent of you to say so," Vivian said cooly.

"Perhaps it is," Stevens agreed. His grin vanished as he glanced at the easel. "I see you've taken my advice."

The man's gaze lingered on the fairy figure, then fell on

Vivian, sitting in the clover with an ease and grace She fumbled to her feet, snatching up her hat.

"Forgive me for staring," the redhead said. "I'm rather fond of your brother's Diana."

"You mean the goddess Diana?" Vivian stared.

The redhead nodded. "The bow and arrow are missing, of course, but she suits you well with her crown of thorns."

"I envisioned her more a fairy than a huntress," Jake admitted.

"The eyes are too much the huntress for a fluttery fairy."

"That was not my intention," Jake mumbled.

"Have you seen it yet, Miss Alderdice?" Stevens asked.

"It's rude to look at an artist's unfinished work unless he permits it." She looked at him with sharp eyes.

"You're quite right," the man agreed. "I was telling Jake yesterday that someone once told me I nose about where it's the least prudent."

"A nasty habit of 'walking into other people's private moments,'" Jake said dryly.

"*Someone* told you that?" She eyed the redhead.

He was quiet as a bird screeched across the sky. "I don't deny it was a woman," he said. "Not the sort you would approve of, Miss Alderdice."

"If she had the sauce to point out a man's flaws, I'd like very much to meet her," said Vivian.

The man roared with laughter. "Perhaps I shall introduce you one day. Come see what your brother has made of you."

She peered over Jake's shoulder. Her mild agitation faded into something more disturbed. "You painted a child!"

"That's precisely what makes it so charming, Miss Alderdice." Stevens insisted.

His sister recovered her composure. "I just didn't expect it." She "Shall we go, Jake? Mother's expecting us for the boat races, you know."

"I'll go back with you," said the redhead. Vivian hardly looked pleased

When they reached the path of red dirt. Vivian stood looking up the hill with a sagging face.

"You've been here before." Stevens studied her.

"Some places carry vivid memories, Mr. Stevens," she said briskly. "But we must not follow false paths."

"What vivid memories, Viv?" Jake asked in a tender voice.

Vivian paused, looking up the hill again. "Brandywine."

"They abandoned the place a long time ago," he reminded her.

Stevens began walking up the hill. "I heard that too, but I'd like to see for myself. I'm rather fond of ghost towns."

Vivian grabbed Jake's hand. "Let's get out of here."

He peered at her. "I want to see what it looks like."

"No!" She grasped his hand. "Some things, once locked, ought to stay locked."

"Why?" He asked, blinking at her. Her eyes were wide. He took her arm, saying in a soothing voice, "Don't be afraid, Viv."

She followed him, her steps reluctant. By the time they reached the top of the hill, they were both panting. Brandywine was now little more than a ghost town. The path heaved with dirty leaves from past rain storms. Huts stood deserted, no smoke coming out of the chimneys and no flowers growing in the gardens.

"It must have been rather lively once," Jake remarked.

His sister's face looked tired. "Once it had a vibrant future. There were even children here. Hope, gratitude and — love." She touched a drawing of three angels on the fence. Jake couldn't help wondering if the memories that plagued her were her own or someone else's.

CHAPTER 9

Jake saw little of Stevens for several weeks after that. Sometimes he would catch glimpses of him, but the redhead was always occupied with his young charges. He wanted to speak with the man, to ask for the help he had promised on the train. But Stevens never caught his eye. The man who had been so affable and interested in his art the first few days in Waxwood now seemed elusive.

He was determined to speak to Stevens and break down the wall that had come between them. After dinner, he fell behind the crowd that headed toward the ballroom for dance his mother and Mrs. Griffith had organized, but lingered in the lobby. The college boys emerged from the dining room and left the hotel. He followed a safe distance behind.

The sea picked up the breeze, catching the hollows of his face and brushing sand in his eyes. People flooded the boardwalk, and he had to move out of the way of billowing skirts and raised parasols as ladies held on to men's arms. He followed the young men to The York, a hotel that catered to middle-class families. The lobby screamed of bright blue and green furnishings. Children ran about while their elders chatted in loud voices, their laughter floating out to the sea. Jake cringed as he saw two young men summoning two giggling young ladies with a shrill whistle.

He followed the college boys down a staircase hidden by a narrow door. At the foot of the stairs was another door marked *Men's Lounge*. Billiards and small tables spread with playing cards crowded the room. A bar containing crystal glasses and decanters lay on a long table. The college boys began pouring drinks, serving themselves first and then urging others to try their concoctions.

Mr. Howe motioned for him to join. The young man's blond hair and tall, gangly figure impressed Jake as more aristocratic than Stevens' bold shoulders and red hair. Up close, he looked older and more pensive than Jake had first thought. He waved the cocktail shaker in Jake's face. "You could have joined us instead of following us like a sly detective."

"I was looking for Stevens." Jake tried to keep his voice steady.

"I don't blame you for seeking livelier entertainment. A libation?" Mr. Howe poured him a glass. "Mind you, we make it strong."

The drink went down like a lightning bolt in his throat. The alcohol hit him quickly, and he grabbed the edge of the table. The young man smirked. "I warned you."

"Where is your cousin?" Jake's voice rose above the noise.

"What makes you think he wants to see you?"

"What makes you think he doesn't?" Jake growled.

The man shrugged and pointed across the room. "He always sits and watches us like some damnable sage."

"Perhaps he's afraid you'll do something foolish." Jake eyed him.

The young man snorted and turned back to the drinks.

He felt as if he were making his way through a fog as he carefully threaded between the smoking men, muttering apologies. The redhead stood in the corner, one shoulder against the wall.

He grinned. "You'll live a charmed life, friend. I was just thinking about you and your Diana. Do you believe in prophecies?"

"I'm not sure."

"I don't know my Bible very well," Stevens confessed, "but I believe there is something there about living to one hundred when one appears while in another's thoughts."

Jake couldn't help but smile. "That's more superstition than holy scripture."

"I see you do know your Bible." His face grew somber. "My father was a rebel of the Catholic church. He was content to give the whole thing up when he came to America. I never set foot in a church." His gaze fell on the liquor table. "Roger thinks I'm bound to hell for it. Whiskey and soda?"

"I've just had one of your cousin's cocktails."

"And your gut is on fire, I take it." Stevens grimaced. "I'm not surprised. They once had a contest who could make the strongest drink, and Roger won." He left him in the corner but returned a few minutes later with the drink.

Jake looked him in the eye. "I've sought you out because I had the impression you were avoiding me."

The redhead bowed. "Not intentionally. I've been preoccupied."

"With your brood?' Jake asked dryly, glancing at the liquor table.

Without answering Stevens asked, "What's on your mind?"

"You promised you would help me with my career," Jake reminded him. "On the train."

"So I did, so I did," said the man. "And I keep my promises." Two men vacated chairs near them. "What have you been doing since the Diana painting?" The redhead settled in.

"I haven't had much chance to do any painting," Jake blushed. "I've had social obligations."

"I can understand that," said Stevens. "I have vivid memories of being pulled from one engagement to the next when I was your age in the name of 'social obligation.'"

"I'm sure you were less awkward at it than I am," Jake remarked.

"My mother wanted it," said Stevens. "My father doesn't give much of a damn about society. He thinks a man ought to find his own society." Stevens put down his empty glass. "You play billiards?"

"Some," Jake said. "I'm not very good."

"I'll lend you some instruction, then." Stevens took his arm.

He really did not play well. He never mastered the proper posture, and the balls were always just missing their target. Mr. Howe and his friends gathered in a circle to watch the game, which only made Jake more skittish. "I don't think they like me," he remarked.

"They envy you," Stevens said. "You're just about to take your position in life. They're still school boys."

"They're lucky to have you to look after them this summer."

The redhead bent toward the shot, spilling two balls in the pockets and earning an impressed murmur from the college boys. "My intention is more than just looking after them."

"I rather thought they were," Jake murmured.

"I have these whims," said Stevens. "Benevolent whims, you might say." He grinned. "One afternoon, they were in the garden at Neart Castle—"

"Neart Castle?" Jake asked.

"Mine and Roger's home," said the redhead. "I was watching their rough play and thinking, 'now, wouldn't it be masterful to teach them to be gentlemen?' The idea came to me to invite them to join me in Waxwood for the summer."

"You invited them?"

"Paying all their expenses," said the man. "I told you I have benevolent whims."

"Was your offer to help me a benevolent whim too?"

Stevens' eyes dimmed. "I'm as serious about helping you as you are about your painting."

Jake leaned against his stick. "I didn't mean to offend you."

"No offense taken, friend." The redhead grinned.

"How can you help me, then?" asked Jake.

Stevens held the cue stick like a pointer. "The first rule of success is to know the right people. I know the right people for *you*."

One of the college boys found a baseball under a table, and they began tossing it between them. Stevens motioned for Mr. Howe. Jake couldn't hear what the redhead whispered in his ear, but Mr. Howe was clearly either annoyed or distressed. He returned to his friends and a few minutes later, they began their own game of billiards.

"Sometimes Roger forgets his manners," Stevens growled. "He's too fond of his outdoor sports."

"Baseball serves the mind better than billiards," Roger snapped. "Football is even better."

Stevens looked at him with hard eyes. "Billiards favors wily intelligence over brute force."

"Competitive sports build strength of mind too, Harland."

Stevens set aside his stick. "That may be, but the fact remains that no one was ever killed in the billiard room."

"No one's ever been killed in *our* games," flared his cousin.

"I'm glad to hear it." The redhead said. "There are outdoor sports equal to those you favor that take more wily and cunning."

"Such as?" Mr. Howe leaned against the billiard table.

"There is no better sport to develop one's intelligence than hunting."

The young man's face grew sardonic. "Hunting is the most savage game of all."

"Hunting is the most character-building sport of all," the redhead counted. "Only men of character take it up. Perhaps that's why you despise it." Mr. Howe's face turned pale, and he turned back to his game.

"You shouldn't goad him," said Jake quietly. "He has a right to his own interests."

Stevens grinned. "Ever heard of an art critic named Culver?"

Jake remembered reading the hard-lined reviews of artists in the *Sacramento Tribune* several years ago. He nodded.

"He now owns a gallery here in town," the man continued. "He's also one of the most respected men in the art world in California."

"A friend of my sister's suggested I see if any of the galleries here are interested in my work." Jake's hands shook a little, but he managed to sink the ball he was aiming at into the pocket.

"I wouldn't do that, if I were you," said the redhead. "Not yet." The last shot gave Stevens the win, and the game was over.

"What do you advise, then?" Jake put away his stick.

"Show them to Culver instead," said Stevens. "He can give you an expert opinion and guide you as to what you can do next."

"I doubt he would agree to see my work," Jake remarked.

The redhead led him to the other side of the now quiet room. "I'll make the appointment for you."

"You'd be asking an awful lot of the fellow, Stevens."

The man gave him a knowing look. "He owes my father a few favors."

"I don't want to impose on him." Jake pressed his hands together.

The redhead gazed at him. "The second rule of success is don't waste your time on anything or anyone that isn't worth your time. Culver can tell you if you're wasting your time"

Jake stared into the fire that someone had lit while they were playing. The yellow flames danced into a devilish grin. "Thank you, Stevens."

The man gave him a quiet smile freshly conceived from a blank mind.

few days later, a long envelope appeared with the morning mail addressed to him. Inside, Stevens had placed a letter of introduction to Culver and also included a note telling Jake he had arranged the meeting at Culver's gallery for eleven o'clock this coming Sunday. "That ought to give you sufficient time to absolve your soul at church," the redhead wrote.

Jake felt dazed as they walked the few blocks to a chalk-colored building. The Tishers seemed to take their day of worship seriously, as they kept their noses buried in their Bibles until the minister appeared. Marvina waved at them from the back, but his mother gave her only a curt greeting and led them to the front rows to sit with the Griffiths. A haze wrapped itself around him as he listened to the minister thunder about Paul and John and cleansing one's sins.

Afterward he waited with Vivian as their mother lingered to chat with the Tishers. Mr. Howe, dressed in a modest suit befitting the occasion, hurried down the church steps, his hand clutching a worn wooden box with a gold latch. The man mumbled an apology as he bumped into him, his voice polite and subdued. He took his hat off and bowed to Vivian.

"I see you're the only pious one of your lot," she remarked.

"I believe in my God, miss," he said with surprising seriousness.

Jake couldn't help but feel a little self-righteous. "Sin first, then worship, eh, Mr. Howe?"

The young man winced.

"I see you've brought your own personal worship book," Vivian glanced down at the Bible in his hands.

"It belonged to my mother, miss."

Her countenance softened. "I didn't mean to be glib. May I see it?"

He hesitated, but Jake could see he was affected by her obvious compassion, and handed her toe box. The book was etched with gold leaves and secured with a braid of gold clasp.

"It's a lovely gift." She carefully securing the box and returning it to him.

"She left me with the grace of God, for which I will be eternally grateful." The young man said.

"Is it grace or duty?" Jake asked. "They're not the same thing, are they?"

"Some prefer to worship gods and not idols, Mr. Alderdice," the young man snapped.

"Are you referring to your cousin as an idol?"

"Heaven forbid!"

"You're not fond of him, then." Vivian eyed Mr. Howe.

The man hunched his shoulders. "He's done a lot for me, miss. So has his father."

"Stevens is benevolent like a good father," Jake said.

A strange look came on the young man's face. "You really believe that, don't you?"

"Why shouldn't I?" Jake's voice was stubborn in the quiet entrance of the church. "He's helping me with my career without my having asked him."

"Harland has helped other young men in their careers," said Mr. Howe. "They never asked for it either."

"What are you getting at, Mr. How?" Jake glared at him.

"It's how he makes worshipers out of them." Mr. Howe smiled ironically.

"He believes in me as an artist," Jake insisted.

"So it seems," said Mr. Howe. "I saw the letter to Mr. Culver."

"He owns a gallery in town," Jake explained to his sister. "He's a very influential man."

"How does he know Mr. Culver?" asked Vivian.

"He doesn't," said Mr. Howe. "My uncle does. Both of them have a way of making others do things for them, whether or not the other person wants to do them."

"You just told us he's done much for you," Jake remarked. "It's a shame you have so little regard for him."

Mr. Howe's did not seem offended. "I was once very appreciative until I realized the price was too high. Perhaps someday you'll see that too." He bowed to Vivian, and bounded down the stairs.

"You were cruel to him," his sister said.

"He's cruel to his cousin," said Jake.

"He may have spoken crudely about Mr. Stevens, but his intentions toward you were sincere."

"Sincere!"

"He was trying to warn you not to trust Mr. Stevens, Jake," she said.

"I'm well aware what he was trying to do!"

"I think he was really saying his cousin always gets what he's after," continued Vivian. "And he doesn't always get it in a virtuous way."

He glanced at the watch in his vest pocket. "I've found nothing in Stevens' behavior to make me think he isn't virtuous."

"There are people who do that," she lamented. "They seem

philanthropic, but they really are clever at getting what they want whenever they want it and damn the consequences. Our grandfather was one."

"Really, Viv! I think you're being too harsh on both Stevens and Grandfather."

"I believe Mr. Howe." Her voice was heavy with worry.

"I don't," said Jake.

"Still, I think you ought to be careful of him, dear." Her eyes softened.

At that moment, their mother parted from the Griffiths and they walked back to the hotel in silence.

He collected the landscape painting he had done his first morning in Waxwood and the Diana painting, along with a third painting he had done in the wax wood forest. As he slipped down to the lobby, he caught sight of Stevens on the croquet lawn. The redhead caught his eye and, smiling, motioned for him to come out. Jake held the paintings, wrapped carefully in brown paper.

"Don't be nervous, friend," Stevens said. "You've more to offer Culver than he has to offer you."

"Is that the third rule of success?" Jake asked with a timid smile.

The redhead patted him on the back. "You listen closely to my advice. I wish Roger did."

The mention of his cousin gave Jake a sinking feeling. "Wish me luck?"

"My father says a man makes his own luck." Stevens peered at Jake. "Are you really as anxious as all that?"

"It might be only one man's opinion," said Jake. "But it's the first and maybe the only one I'll ever receive."

"Culver can be a little impassive, but he's not a cruel man," said the redhead.

Jake's eyes fell on the college boys. They looked bored and annoyed. Mr. Howe was not among them.

Stevens grinned. "I'm trying to teach them the game."

"They don't seem to take to it," Jake remarked.

"I expect they have more tolerance for their lectures," the redhead agreed.

"Then why bother?"

"Call it a test, if you wish." The man glanced at them.

"A test of what?"

Stevens gave him an odd smile. "One you would pass without a doubt, friend."

Jake picked up his paintings. "I saw Roger at church this morning."

The man's face wrinkled. "Roger takes the whole business of religion seriously. It's the only thing in life to which he devotes himself with earnestness." He studied the edge of his mallet. "What else did Roger say of me?"

Jake said in a hurried tone, "He told us nothing important."

"Us?" The man's eyes were keen.

"Vivian was there."

Stevens face deepened with lines. "I don't know as I like that. No, I don't like that at all."

As Jake made his way to the desk, Mr. Howe emerged, having changed from the solemn brown suit he had worn at church to a brighter one with the insignia pinned to his lapel. He had none of the animosity of that morning's encounter and looked, in fact, as if he had forgotten the incident. "May I see them?" His tone was solemn and curious as he looked down at the paintings.

Though Jake would have liked more than anything to refuse, his good breeding forbade it. The young man lingered on them with thoughtful eyes, then bound them again with care before handing them to Jake. "Perhaps you were right this morning about Harland. Perhaps this is a more authentic interest of his." He held out his hand."Good luck."

Jake shook the young man's hand. "I'd like to apologize for my conduct this morning."

An uncertain glance flickered on his face. "I only hope what I said does you some good someday." Without another word, he went off to join his friends.

CHAPTER 11

Jake lingered for a few moments in the lobby after Mr. Howe had gone. The place was quiet at that late hour of the morning. Some people were just returning from church services, and their eyes scanned him as he stood with his paintings.

"Would you be kind enough to tell me where I could find Culver's Gallery?" he asked a young woman at the desk.

"Yes, sir," she said. "It's in the recent development."

"Where is that?"

She came up with a crudely drawn map of Waxwood, showing him how to reach Vine Street, the new road expanding from the resorts. "It's quite an ostentatious place, sir," The young woman was clearly proud of her extended vocabulary.

He made his way past the hotels. Small shops with Swiss trimmed roofs and polished white doors gave the feeling of a European village. Everything was where it ought to be without a speck of grime. Each establishment hung a whitewashed sign swinging on two gold chains, so when they rocked in the wind, they reminded him of ladies' fans flapping back and forth at a ball. These were establishments meant for people of leisure such as himself — restaurants, tea shops, and art galleries.

Mr. Culver stood outside Culver's Gallery, an impressive building with two large windows. He looked more like a scientist than a man with a passion for art. His hands clasped behind him, and large spectacles obliterated his eyes. He greeted Jake without smiling, and his eyes remained impassive as he read Stevens' letter.

"It was most kind of you to agree to see my work, Mr. Culver," Jake began.

"Mr. Stevens has indomitable powers of persuasion." The man folded the letter and returned it to Jake.

Jake shuddered as he remembered Vivian's words: *He always gets what he's after.* "Thank you all the same," he mumbled.

"I'm not usually here on a Sunday," the little man grumbled. Then, he softened. "However, I'm always happy to see a new artist's work."

Jake leaned the paintings against the wall. All his bones seemed ready to fall from their joints as he waited for Mr. Culver's verdict.

"You've had some training, I take it?"

Jake nodded. "From James Magwich."

He could see the glint in Mr. Culver's eyes. "He's a fine master of technique."

"Before that, my grandmother taught me," Jake continued. "She was an artist too."

"Her name?"

"Penelope Alderdice." Then, he remembered Bertha Ross and her ramblings. "I mean, Grace Carlyle."

"And where did she show her work?"

"Nowhere," Jake admitted. "She did some work here in Waxwood, though."

Mr. Culver's manner became less high-tone. "I heard some fine artists came out of Brandywine."

"I don't think she was at Brandywine," said Jake. "She was staying with friends."

"That was perhaps lucky for her," the man remarked. "I heard the colony had fine ideals, but not much regard for the market. Reality must come in the artist's way. Always."

"I realize that, Mr. Culver," said Jake. "That's why I came to you."

The gallery owner was pleased and studied the paintings more in earnest. Jake would have liked more than anything to remove his gloves at that moment, as his hands were clammy underneath.

The man's look was not entirely noncommittal, and Jake detected a shadow of compassion. "An interesting interpretation of these local woods."

"You've been there?" Jake asked.

"No," he admitted. "I recognize them, of course. Every person with an any artistic sense who visits Waxwood either composes a poem about them or paints them."

Jake's heart sank. "You're not impressed, then."

Mr. Culver glanced outside the window. "I am impressed with how you transformed those woods into something uncommon. You've more spirit than other young artists I've met."

"But?"

"As I said before, the realities of the market must always come in the artist's way."

"What do you mean, sir?"

"I mean fantastic forest scenes won't sell, Mr. Alderdice."

"There are artists who paint as I do," Jake pointed out. "Mr. Stevens told me about the Symbolists."

"They're in Europe, son," said Mr. Culver. "American prefer more tangible art." He opened a small door. "If you care to look, I'm sure it will become clearer to you."

The room was a small, illuminating statues and paintings on display. It did not take him long to see what Mr. Culver meant.

Every landscape and portrait looked ready to come to life at any moment. "Tangible art," Jake murmured. "Diana, not he other hand, is an illusive creature."

Mr. Culver's owl expression looked almost regrettable. "Those are the realities of the market now."

"Then there's little point in trying to sell my paintings in America," Jake said.

The man hesitated. "You might go abroad and study a little more."

Jake pressed his hands together. "To what end, Mr. Culver?"

The man removed his glasses again. "Perhaps you're right. It's not technique you're missing in your work, son. Nor is it imagination."

"It's talent." Jake let the word drop.

The man cleared his throat. "Your details are exacting, there's no question about that. The features on the girl, the shape of the trees, the salamanders—"

"Mr. Culver," Jake interrupted, "I came here hoping to gain some insights into my work. I ask you to speak to me plainly."

"I don't say there isn't *something* in your work," the man hedged.

"But that's not enough."

"Not for a career, no." The man put his hand on Jake's wrist. "One needs a broad audience for a career."

Jake was stifled, and he wanted to smash the two perfect windows so he could breathe again. He gathered his paintings. "The best I can hope for, then, is to please myself."

Mr. Culver smiled. "That is not a bad end, Mr. Alderdice."

Jake couldn't see the white walls around him or Mr. Culver. He saw leafy green, red bark, a flash of blue from a bird's feathers. He saw himself, a gawky, lanky child clutching a paintbrush in his hand, an unsmiling child. Numb realization replaced the warmth and truth the child had felt. "I could go to the other galleries," he said under his breath. "Get other opinions." But he knew others would have none of the compassion or honesty of this man who spent many hours looking at the work of young artists. "Thank you, Mr. Culver."

"I encourage you to consider going to Europe nonetheless," the man said.

"I have nothing to give others," said Jake. "I would be wasting my time. Fiddling my life away," he added, feeling his throat close.

"Aren't you exaggerating?" The man asked gently.

"My grandfather wouldn't have thought so," Jake lamented. "He wouldn't have wanted me to invest my life in a fruitless endeavor. I shall have to try something else." He held out his hand. "I thank you again, sir."

Mr. Culver took his hand in both of his for a moment. "You've accepted this with grace, son. I don't see that often in a young man your age. Rest assured those qualities will serve you well." He bowed and withdrew through the small door.

When Jake was far away from the gallery, he let his head drop and the tears come.

CHAPTER 12

Jake hid in his room the rest of that day, staring at the paint box and palette lying in the corner. His sister peered through the door to take him to dinner but he shook his head. He was grateful she did not press him but only gave a sorrowful nod and closed the door.

He came into the lobby rather late. Rain grated the hotel roof and the wind pressed into the French doors. Nevertheless, he went to the York.

The men's lounge was crowded, the billiard and card tables occupied, and conversations amplified with loud laughter. Stevens sat in a corner near the window watching the college boys play billiards, his large hand grasping a cigar. His lips were thin, and his eyes dimmed with brooding.

Jake approached him. "You look like you need a drink."

The man grimaced as he cast a wary eye around the smoky room. "Why don't we go to my suite? Much more pleasant there, and the liquor is better." He threw the cigar in the plate on the small table beside him. "When the smoke clears, the air here will filthy with mendacity, mark my words." He sighed. "Forgive me. I'm a little despondent tonight."

"They say listening to someone else's troubles is a proper remedy for your own," Jake remarked.

The man laughed. "I don't doubt it, friend." He gave Jake an inquisitive look. "Are you interested in books?"

"Not as much as my sister," he said.

"Perhaps I can tempt you with some of my rare books, then. Ah, pure air at last!" He breathed in the damp air. "Air cures mendacity and despondency both."

Stevens' suite had none of the ornate qualities of the Alderdice suite. Rather than heavy maple and walnut, the redhead's suite ceramic and glass filled the rooms, making the place brighter and breezier.

"You approve of the Nouveau decor?" The redhead produced a crystal decanter and glasses. "It hurls one into the modern world, doesn't it?" His eyes were a little hooded as he handed Jake the drink. Jake wondered how much he had been drinking that evening.

"To new beginnings." Jake raised his glass.

Stevens spread his arm across the back of the empty seat beside him. "Is this new philosophy a result of your visit with Culver this afternoon?"

Jake took a chair with clean lines. "Mr. Culver doesn't believe I can be a successful painter."

"I know." The man's voice was quiet. "He told me all about it."

"Then you don't need me to tell you anything." Jake put the glass down and rose.

The redhead's hand shot out. "I'm interested in what you have to say."

Jake sat down again. "I do not paint the tastes of the current market, and, therefore, I'm painting for myself alone."

"I'm sure he didn't say that."

"Not in so many words," Jake admitted. "But it amounts to the same thing. He recommended I go to Europe."

"Well, why don't you?"

"It would be a waste of time," he insisted. "That would make me a idler, and that's the last thing my grandfather wanted."

They were silent for a while, the sea buzzing outside. "So you see, I'm as despondent as you are."

"Oh, no, friend," said Stevens with a strange laugh. "My despondency is the most shattering one may encounter."

"And what is your despondency, Stevens?"

"Mendacity in all her glory," the man growled.

"You seem fond of that word tonight," Jake remarked.

The redhead leaned forward. "Do you know what it really means?"

"Lying," Jake said.

"It's more than that," said Stevens. "A man is embraces mendacity with his whole heart, not just his words. Like Mr. Culver."

"Culver was very truthful with me," Jake insisted.

"One may speak the truth and still be living with lies," said the redhead. "When cloaked in honest opinion, well, mendacity is just another one of Pierrot's pranks."

"Men say such things when they've been disheartened by a woman," Jake remarked.

This made the redhead roar with laugher. "Columbine disheartened Pierrot, didn't she? But, no, it isn't always a woman." He sighed and poured another drink. "When one puts one's faith in youth and they fail, that can be more disheartening than a woman's scorn."

Jake at last understood. "You mean your cousin and his friends."

Stevens slammed the glass on the table. "They're gluttony for idleness is as insatiable as your abhorrence of it."

"They'll calm down when they finish their studies," Jake said politely.

"I wouldn't be too sure of that." He bounded toward the bedroom and emerged a few moments later, balancing a book in his hands. "The godfather of the Transcendentalists." His voice boomed with strange excitement.

"Who are they?"

"They, friend, are our spiritual godfathers." The man's voice was harsh and gritty. "And this book is about the quest for purity. Henry David Thoreau spent two years in a small cottage by a pond to prove to the world the mendacity of modern life's pleasures."

Jake's hand moved toward the beautiful book, but Stevens grabbed his hand away. "Don't touch it!"

"I'm sorry," Jake murmured. "I should have realized it was valuable."

The redhead's fingers loosened. "I didn't hurt you, did I?"

"No, of course not," Jake lied.

"What lies between the pages is more of value than its age."

"Perhaps I'll let you read it one day." The man promised. He sat down again, his mild tone returned. "What do you intend to do now?"

Jake shrank back. "I was hoping you could advise me."

Stevens leaned back "You come seeking a father's wisdom. I like that."

"I come to you as a friend."Jake said firmly. "I told you I didn't need a father,"

Stevens looked hard at him. "I often wonder why you young men look for strife when there are often more assured roads of success right at your disposal."

"Because sometimes we have our own dreams that differ from what our family wants," Jake mumbled. "You were referring to my grandfather's shipping business, weren't you?"

"You have a quick mind, friend," said Stevens, smiling. "Well, why not the shipping business?"

"Why not indeed," Jake said. "It would appease my grandfather's ghost. All the ghosts, in fact."

"You're being morbid, aren't you?"

"It's Vivian's idea, not mine," he insisted. "My sister believes in family specters."

"The Scottish believe in ghosts and legends, too," Stevens lamented. "I had a nanny from Glasgow who used to tell me stories about them until my father found out about it."

"He believes in legends as much as he does in religion," Jake surmised.

"He believes in what he can see and touch. And so do I." The redhead took the glasses and refilled them. "So should you from now on."

"I was looking at my paints just now," Jake mused. "They didn't seem real."

They sat silent for a while as the waves crashed outside. Jake opened the drapes all the way. Yellow stars illuminated the blue sky like little eyes peering at him. Not even the water was visible, nor the beach itself. If he only opened the windows, nothing would stop him from diving in.

CHAPTER 13

The lobby was unusually quiet when Jake returned to the Waxwoodian. His melancholy had cleared with the sifting sea air. The elevator boy, who could become chatty when he was alone, remarked, "Won't go out when there's rain, sir. Like it was fire or somethin'."

"Rain is a blessing," Jake murmured.

"That's jus' what I think, sir!" The boy grinned as he slid the elevator doors open. "My old grandma used to say so too."

Jake gave him a raw smile. "So did mine." As he walked down the quiet hallway, he mused, "Not so very different, an Alderdice and an elevator boy."

His mother and sister sat across from one another, a pot of cocoa on the table between them. He could tell they were in the middle of an argument, as they were both looking moody and agitated. His sister glanced tried to smile when he entered the room, but her eyes were tight. His mother did not notice as he helped himself to a cup of the cocoa and slipped into a stuffy chair in the corner.

Larissa gave Vivian one of her seething looks. "I made it very clear you were to stay away from that woman, Vivian."

"Marvina is my friend, Mother." Vivian's jaw was rigid.

"A friend would hardly drag you to such a filthy place —"

"It was a meeting about the future of the women in this country," Vivian said. "You went to a suffragist meeting?" Jake stared at her.

"And I assure you, there were plenty of blue bloods there," said his sister. "It's quite the fashion now to court progressives."

"You are not a progressive!"

"Is there anything wrong with forward-thinking?" He lamented. "One must forge ahead, mustn't one?"

His mother glanced at him. "Go to bed, Jacob. This doesn't concern you."

He sat up. "You tried to order me to bed once, remember?" His mother winced as if recalling the night of his grandmother's funeral when he refused to leave while Vivian confronted her about Bertha Ross. "It didn't work then, and it won't work now!"

Larissa turned to Vivian again. "*Decent* blue bloods avoid such people."

"Marvina supports them, and she's decent," Vivian pointed out. "She would have been ousted out of Washington Street a long time ago if she weren't."

"I'm not so sure she won't be," his mother remarked. "Even Mrs. Griffith has noticed she's become entirely too radical in her views lately, and Mrs. Griffith is quite tolerant."

"Mrs. Griffith tolerant?" Jake couldn't help but laugh.

"Radicals have no respect for traditions," said his mother. "No sense of responsibility or honor."

"What do you consider responsible and honorable?" Vivian regarded Larissa with some amusement. "A young girl uniting with some worn-out businessman, bearing his children, and exhausting herself with social obligations?"

"Viv, you're twisting the knife," Jake murmured.

"I often wonder," his sister continued, "whether you didn't marry knowing you would be widowed sooner rather than later.

A rather ingenious way of fulfilling one's womanly duty and gaining one's freedom at the same time."

"Vivian!"

"I rather agree with Marvina. If social propriety hadn't distorted your wit and intelligence, you might have achieved something in this world."

Larissa rose, her features stiff. Jake wondered whether she intended to slap Vivian. But she only said, "I'm tired and I want to go to bed. But fist, I want your promise you won't attend one of those meetings again."

"I can't make any more promises, Mother."

"You have a mutinous streak, Vivian," Larissa said gently. "I'm only trying to help you."

"Don't worry, Mother. No blue blood woman ever strayed far from conformity." His sister's voice was wary.

"Conventional life has its rewards," his mother reminded her. "Comfort and peace of mind, for one."

"Yes, that's true, isn't it?" Jake thought of Stevens. "Why look for strife when there are more assured paths?"

"You forgot to mention expectations," Vivian said. "Do you know what Grandmother thought of expectations? She thought they were like a stone necklace choking one's throat."

"Your grandmother had a mutinous streak too," said Larissa. "But she tamed it, and she went very far." His mother looked at her with steady eyes. "I ask little of you or your brother. I'm asking you to do this."

He looked at his mother's drab pallor and realized it was not a mere trick of the light. She was, in fact, terrified.

Vivian sat down on the chair. "All right, Mother. I promise."

"And you'll keep *this* promise?" Larissa persisted.

Vivian nodded, but Jake knew too well the glint in her eyes that read *for now*.

Larissa stepped into the hallway.

"Wait, Mother!" He jumped up. "I've something to tell you."

She looked over her shoulder. "I said I was tired, Jacob."

"You'll want to hear this," he said. "It concerns my future and the future of the family."

Larissa's eyebrows peaked with interest as she returned to the couch.

"I went to see a man named Culver today," said Jake. "He owns a gallery in town."

"Is that what Mr. Howe was referring to this morning?" Vivian put her cup carefully on the table.

Jake nodded. "Stevens gave me the letter of introduction."

His mother looked even more interested. "I'm glad you took the initiative, Jacob. Is he going to buy your paintings?"

"I went to get his opinion, Mother," he said. "Stevens thought it would be best that way."

"Did he?" Vivian raised an eyebrow.

"I'm sure Mr. Stevens knows better than we do, Vivian," said his mother. "What was Mr. Culver's opinion?"

Jake fiddled with a silver spoon. "I've a keen eye for detail but will probably never have true success."

His mother was silent. His sister said, "Who is he to say such a thing to you?"

"He was a successful art critic before he owned his gallery," said Jake. "He knows what he's talking about, Viv."

"Did he say anything else?" asked Larissa in a calm voice.

"He suggested I go to Europe to study," said Jake.

Vivian smiled. "You see, Mother, Marvina knew what she was talking about."

His mother peered at him. "Do you want to go?"

He felt his throat go dry. "It would do no good."

"Nonsense!" Vivian said. "Mr. Culver clearly thinks you need more instruction."

"It was a concession, Viv," Jake said in a sour voice.

"But you're devoted to art!" his sister insisted.

Jake glared at the spoon. "Devotion doesn't make an artist, Viv."

"What do you intend to do now?" Larissa asked.

He took a deep breath. "I'll be going into Alderdice Shipping when we return to the city."

He could see Vivian go from flushed anger to surprise. His mother smiled with obvious satisfaction.

"I shall start at the bottom, of course, just as you said," he continued. "I'm sure Alex Runyan will teach me what I need to know."

"Mr. Runyan will do what's necessary," his mother assured him. "Your grandfather had prepared him for this."

Jake gave a tight smile. "This ought to satisfy Grandfather."

"And you, Mother," Vivian said in a quiet voice. "You ought to be satisfied too."

Larissa's eyes were a penetrating blue, just as his grandfather's had been. Her face was smooth and her lips slack with emotion. She rose and laid a hand on his arm. "I know you'll do the family proud. " Her voice was soothing. "You'll do *them* proud."

"Jake, you can't be serious about all this!" Vivian sat up.

"Leave your brother alone," said Larissa. "He knows what he wants."

"It isn't what he wants, it's what you and Grandfather want!" Vivian snapped.

"It's what I want, Viv," he said.

In a resolute tone, Larissa asked, "Shall I telegram Mr. Runyan in the morning and let him know to expect you in September?" He nodded. "Good night, then." As she went into the hallway, she looked over her shoulder at Vivian. "Remember, dear, I expect you to use sound judgment about your life just as your brother has."

"Sound judgment!" Vivian snarled after she had gone.

"Your judgement is sound when you try," Jake insisted.

"Whose judgment are you going by?" Vivian eyed him. "Your own or Mr. Stevens?"

His looked away. "Let it alone, Viv."

"This sudden desire of yours to fulfill family expectations came from him, didn't it?"

"His judgment is sound too." Jake pressed his fingers together.

She sat on the arm of his chair. "Is it, dear? Is it really?"

His anger rose. "I won't fritter away my time in Europe with nothing to show for it. Every man must find his own destiny."

Vivian was silent, looking out the balcony at the night spilling into the room. "Do you really believe it's your destiny to become a shipping tycoon?"

"Why not?" He insisted. "It was Grandfather's, wasn't it?"

"But it isn't what you really want, is it?"

"What does it matter?" He raised his voice. "I won't be fiddling with life. That's the important thing."

"Even if you might end up miserable?"

"I won't be," he said. "I'll be comfortable and peaceful, just as Mother said." He yawned. "I'm going to bed."

His sister grasped his arm, her fingers taking into his skin. "Put off your decision until the fall," she pleaded. "Give yourself time to think, really think."

He gave her a wary look. "You once told me younger brothers don't give advice to older sisters. The opposite is true too."

"And I'm giving it to you anyway, just as you gave it to me. Bury yourself in the family business, and you'll kill your passion for art forever."

"It's dead already," Jake said. "Like an imaginary playmate one no longer needs."

She put her arms around him. "You might find you haven't lost your desire to paint if you go."

"It's too late." He gripped her shoulders. "Stevens said he would help me."

"As he helped you with Mr. Culver?" She backed away.

"At least he won't die on me like my own father did," Jake snapped.

It was never easy silencing Vivian, whose tongue snapped up any insinuation, but she did not answer because she couldn't deny the truth of what he said.

CHAPTER 14

Though Jake had told Vivian his interest in painting was gone, he found himself taking up drawing. He made small sketches of real subjects with pencil stubs on bits of paper or envelopes. But the human bodies always ended up looking maniacal. This new direction frightened him, and yes, he couldn't keep his hand from moving.

One afternoon, he wandered out to the croquet lawn and began a game. The hollow knock of the mallet against the ball startled him out of his inertia. He eased a blue ball through the hoop, knocking the green ball away as he did so. He heard a laugh behind him. "Not much good putting through your opponent's ball, is it?" Stevens stood with his hands in his pockets, surveying the green grass.

Jake was silent. He hadn't seen the redhead since their conversation that night in the suite.

"I've reserved the hoops for an hour," Stevens admitted. "I had some vague notion of finding Roger and continuing my lesson with him. He showed some aptitude for the game the last time."

"I thought his mendacious life disgusted you." Jake recalled their strange conversation with a little shudder.

"You mustn't take my moods too seriously." The redhead smiled. "Shall I give you some pointers, as I did with the billiards? You're a good learner, friend."

"My grandmother always taught me to keep my eyes and ears alert,"

"She was right," said the redhead. "It's the best way to learn."

"It wasn't learning she was after," he said. "She thought people revealed themselves when you least expected it."

"Your grandmother must have been an extraordinary woman," said Stevens, his voice sincere.

"She was," Jake murmured.

"Shall we play?" Stevens took off his jacket. Jake laid his on the bench, as he suddenly realized the lawn felt like a hothouse.

The man guided him as he had on the billiard table, but Jake continued to make little fouls, apologizing more than necessary and fiddling with his mallet.

"You seem a little lost, friend," Stevens observed.

"On the contrary, I've found myself." He tapped the ball with the mallet before he shot it, overestimating the swing. "I'm taking your advice."

"Oh?"

"When we return to the city, I shall go into my grandfather's business."

He wasn't sure what he expected. On the boardwalk, two ladies passed holding their hats down to keep them from flying off in the wind. They stopped for a moment and looked at Stevens with inviting smiles. But the man ignored them, and the two ladies hurried away, their heels clanking against the planks.

"I hope I shall prove myself worthy of my family name," Jake added.

"Why wouldn't you?" asked the redhead.

"I don't fool myself, Stevens," he said. "I have no head for business. I don't even have much interest in it."

"That will come in time," Stevens reassured him.

"Whether it does or doesn't hardly matters." Jake's voice broke.

Stevens leaned against his mallet. "I once wanted to be a professional hunter. Traveling the world, bringing back obscure game, that sort of thing. I envisioned myself roaming the great wide open."

"Why didn't you?"

"Because my father insisted I come work at the cannery," said the redhead. "I was eighteen, and the thought of sitting behind a mahogany desk seemed worse than prison to me."

"You never told him about your dream?" Jake asked softly.

"He wanted me in the cannery, and no one ever contradicts him." A hint of bitterness crept into his usually bland voice. "He gave me one concession, though. He let me choose what I wanted to do. I chose to go down into the factory where the Chinese cleaned and gutted the fish."

"That was brave of you," said Jake.

He shot the ball through two hoops. "It turned out to be very educational. I learned a little Chinese philosophy from the men there."

"And your father wasn't furious with you?"

"He came down every day to watch me work in my bloodied apron and rubber gloves," said Stevens.

"He must have been proud of you," Jake said.

Stevens grimaced. "I think he was more curious than anything else. He wanted to see how long I would last it out."

"And how long did you last it out?"

"Three months." The redhead tapped the grass with his mallet. "I told my father I wanted to go into the office. He had a desk already prepared for me." He grinned. "A big desk in a room with plenty of sunshine."

"He knew you would come eventually," Jake guessed.

"He never said a word to reprimanded me," said Stevens. "He understood I had to find out for myself."

The afternoon heat bore down with a vengeance. Jake wiped

at his forehead with his handkerchief. "I suppose your father understood you." He made a shot through the hoop. "I'd like someone to understand me that way."

He felt the weight of the redhead's expectant eyes. "You've changed your mind."

"About what"

"About needing guidance," said the redhead. "Other young men have come to me when they needed a father too."

"I didn't say I needed a father." Jake looked at the tussled grass at his feet. "I only meant I would be grateful for any ideas you have for me."

"As you wish," said Stevens, his eyes sparkling in the sun.

"You can start by telling me the fourth rule of success," Jake said lightly.

"Learn your trade from the ground up," said the man in a grave tone. "Then decide what you'll do and what others will do."

"My grandfather relied on a manager for years," Jake said, thinking of Alex Runyan.

"You must have everything in your control at all times, but only when you're ready," the man advised.

Jake laid the mallet on the grass. "I seem to be forever in your debt, Stevens."

The man plucked his coat from the bench. "You can thank me by buying me a drink."

When they entered the lobby, Jake saw his mother and sister freshly dressed for lunch. Vivian was explaining something to Larissa, but stopped talking when she saw them.

"This is Mr. Stevens, Mother," Jake said. "I told you about him."

Larissa went into her hospitality persona. "A pleasure to meet you, Mr. Stevens."

"Good afternoon, ma'am." The redhead bowed, then turned to Vivian. "How are you, Miss Alderdice?"

"You know my daughter?" His mother's eyes slid toward his sister.

"We had the pleasure of meeting." He crushed the edge of his hat in his hands.

"You should have told me, dear," Larissa said. "Young ladies are so secretive these days."

"Mr. Stevens is Jake's friend, not mine," Vivian said. "I take it your cousin and his friends have been keeping you busy, Mr. Stevens?"

The redhead gave her an ingratiating smile. "I prefer to leave them to their interests."

"You're not educating them, then?" Asked Larissa.

"Here and there," he said. "But I prefer to devote more time to my own pursuits."

"And what are your pursuits, Mr. Stevens?" Vivian asked.

"That's Stevens' business, Viv," Jake said.

"I apologize for my daughter's impertinence," Larissa said. "Vivian's outspokenness sometimes impedes on her manners."

"Mr. Stevens already knows I'm not a shirking rose," countered his sister.

"I find much to admire in that, Miss Alderdice."

Vivian stared at him. "I almost believe you mean that."

"I would rather try to tame a fearless young woman than an idle young man," The redhead murmured.

Vivian gave him a wry smile. "Is that why you've abandoned your efforts with your cousin and his friends?"

"I'm not their teacher, Miss Alderdice." Stevens leaned against an empty chair. "Roger is like a son to me. He grew up in my father's house."

"That's a strange way of putting it," said Vivian. "Most people would say 'we grew up together.'"

"I can hardly say that," the man chuckled. "I'm quite a bit older than he, after all. But we get along well."

Jake remembered the young man's tart words and narrow gaze when he spoke to Stevens, but he said nothing.

"I'll be taking him to the farm tomorrow to get him a dog," Stevens continued. "A man I know. He's quite a character."

"Does he give sell them or give them away?" Vivian asked.

"Why don't you both come and see for yourself?" The redhead glanced at Jake.

"Our grandfather never liked dogs," he said.

"We had a collie when I was a child," Larissa remarked. Both Jake and Vivian stared at her. "He would chase birds in the garden. I don't think he ever caught one."

"Collies wouldn't, ma'am," said Stevens politely. "They're not really bird dogs."

"You seem to know something about the animals, Mr. Stevens." Vivian said.

"I have a deep respect for them."

"I'd like to go," Jake said.

The redhead turned to Vivian. "Miss Alderdice?"

"I don't think so," she said.

"It would do you good to get some fresh air, dear," said Larissa. "You've been far too bookish this summer."

"A ride in the country is just the thing, Viv," Jake urged.

"The place is beautiful," Stevens said. "The farm is quite big, not one of those shabby places with the barn going to ruins."

Vivian glanced at him, then at Stevens. "Why not? We'll see these dogs of yours, Mr. Stevens."

"Perhaps you might even get one yourself," said the redhead with a smile. "My friend might have a lap dog that are partial to ladies."

"I think a guard dog would be more my taste," said Vivian. Her smile looked something like a grinning Medusa.

CHAPTER 15

Stevens met them in the lobby after breakfast the next morning. The college boys came with him, glancing around with uncertainty until Mr. Harrington produced a football, and the young men filed out with their usual enthusiastic ruckus. Jake noticed the envy on Mr. Howe's face.

Vivian remarked, "You look as if you would rather play football than get a dog, Mr. Howe."

"I've always wanted a pet, miss." His usual gruff tone was more refined. "I only wish my friends could help me choose it."

"Rodney would hardly appreciate your friends teasing his dogs," Stevens said.

"They wouldn't do that, Harland," said the young man. His cousin only glared at him.

Stevens was clearly well acquainted with the blacksmith, Mr. Shelley, as they chatted amiably about horses. The blacksmith's seemed wary of Vivian, but his sister lavished her charm upon him. While Stevens and Mr. Howe prepared the wagon, she showed interest in the horses insisting Mr. Shelley introduce her to them all by name. Stevens' admiration for the way she softened this women-wary, middle-aged man was apparent in the smile on his lips.

"You have an intelligent sister," said Mr. Howe.

"It's kind of you to say so."

"I never had much of a family," the young man admitted. "Until Harland's father took me in, that is."

"I'm sorry to hear that, Mr. Howe," said Jake.

"You may as well call me Roger."

As they started out of town, Vivian asked, "I take it you have ample experience with dogs, Mr. Stevens?"

"My father keeps beagles and pit bulls," said the redhead. "Good hunting dogs."

"Is your fondness for dogs because they're as obedient as your young followers?" Vivian raised her parasol over her head.

"On the contrary, Miss Alderdice." Stevens grinned. "One cannot tame a person as one tames a dog."

"You see to have some success," said Vivian. "Since it was you who convinced Jake to give up his art to go into business."

Roger stared with alarm at his cousin.

"No one convinced me to do anything, Viv" Jake snapped.

"What makes you think I convinced him?"

"I know my brother," she said. "I know how long he dreamed of being an artist. You took that away from him."

The redhead gave her a severe look. "Your brother just said I had nothing to do with it, Miss Alderdice."

"You would think that, Harland," Roger turned to Jake. "So you're not going to be an artist after all?"

"That's hardly your business," Stevens snarled.

His cousin shaded his eyes from the sun. "It wasn't yours either."

"I'm beginning to believe were right about the dangers of worshiping idols, Mr. Howe," said Vivian.

The young man stared at the road, his face impenetrable.

"Your cousin had rather astute views on the subject," said

Vivian. "He warned my brother about the danger of following idols."

"Dr. Faustus wanted power," Roger said. "He sold his soul to get it."

"I hardly think Jake would consort with the devil." Deep lines appeared on the redhead's face as they turned a fork in the road.

"One never can tell what one might become, Mr Stevens," Vivian remarked. Something in the redhead's keen gaze told Jake this veiled accusation disturbed him.

The farm was old but pleasant. Chickens and goats wandered the yard looking confused as the visitors entered the gate. The door flew open, and Rodney Stoker bounced out. He was a man with a heavily bearded face over sun-baked skin.

The man grabbed Stevens' hand, giving it a violent shake. "Brought people with you, eh? You know we always enjoy seein' new people. Not much doin' out here." He caught sight of Vivian and took his hat off. "Mornin', miss."

"My cousin would like one of your dogs, sir," said Stevens.

"Well, now, you come at the right time, young man," said the man. "Summer's the time when people go 'way and leave their dogs behind, poor wretches."

"How cruel," Jake remarked.

"Oh, they don't just leave 'em to rot, son," said Mr. Stoker. "They bring 'em to me 'cause they know I'll find 'em a good home." His tone grew serious as he glanced at Stevens. "You vouch for your cousin?"

"Certainly."

He regarded Roger with a suspicious look. "What you aimin' to do with the dog, son?"

"Do?" The young man echoed.

"I don't go givin' my dogs to them that's gonna use 'em for profit," he said. He grew sterner. "I got to know you'll treat it right."

Roger was not without dignity. Jake had to admit Roger could command respect without appearing to be arrogant. "I would never harm a dog, Mr. Stoker, nor any animal."

"Roger's all right, Rod," said the redhead. "We're practically brothers." He put his arm around the young man's shoulders. Roger remained stoic.

"I still gotta ask my questions, Mr. Stevens," said the man. "No offense. What you want the dog for, son?"

"A pet, of course," said Roger.

This response satisfied Mr. Stoker, as the farmer led them through the yard. When they reached the back of the house, he addressed Vivian. "Don't want to alarm you, miss, but dogs can get a little excitable when there's a woman about."

"Mr. Stevens assured me they're not dangerous."

"Oh, nothin' like that, miss. I don't keep them kind of dogs." He rubbed his chin. "But some of 'em's been away from ladies for a long time, even since they were pups. They get kinda skittish when they see a skirt, like boys who've had too much beer on a Sunday night." He guffawed, but then grew pensive. "Might scare you some if you ain't use to it."

"Mr. Stoker, I'm not afraid of a few rambunctious dogs."

"Miss Alderdice is like Diana, Rod," said Stevens.

"Eh?"

"She's more likely to frighten the dogs than they are to frighten her." The redhead grinned. "She's not a woman with whom any male, man or dog, would care to trifle."

Mr. Stoker burst out laughing. "Well, bless your heart, miss. I guess young ladies is like that now'days. Shame my wife's out in the field. The missus is always keen on speakin' with other ladies. Gets kinda lonesome for her here."

"I'm sure it does," Vivian said.

He led them through a field of wild grass until they reached a fenced area with a dozen or so dogs. Some were lying in the shade or stretched out in the sun while a few drank water from a bucket.

Before Jake could stop her, Vivian ran to the edge of the fence. The dogs came to life, running and barking, shoving their muzzles against the wire and wagging their tails. Jake watched with bewilderment as his sister scratched their heads, laughing and cooing at them.

Mr. Stoker gave one of his slapping laughs. "Well, guess that settles that!"

Stevens watched her with a quiet smile, his face more relaxed than Jake had ever seen. Roger was clearly finding the noise irritating as he covered his ears. Mr. Stoker became suddenly business-like as he explained each dog's breed. The young man seemed to have little interest in their pedigree and shouted over the noise, "I just want a dog, blast it!"

"Why not the fox hound, Roger?" His cousin nodded at a lively pup with its begging eyes set upon the newcomers.

"I don't know 'bout that one, Mr. Stevens." The farmer leaned against the fence. "Them fox hounds chase after prey like nobody's business. Got to keep 'em runnin', or they can get vicious."

Roger shrank back. "No thank you, sir."

"You're a great believer in exercise, Roger," Stevens reminded him. "I should hardly think it would be a problem for you to keep a dog active."

"I'd rather not," the young man mumbled.

"Take a look at them spaniels then," said Mr. Stoker. "They're your best bet. Playful, nice dogs. Purty, too." The man winked as he opened the gate and whistled to a spaniel sitting under a tree. It came quickly, but not before a hound and a Saint Bernard squeezed out of the opening and ascended upon Jake, waving their friendly tails and barking their greetings.

"Ain't interested, son?" The man hurried the spaniel through the gate. "Saint Bernards ain't as lively as you'd think, though. Kinda cushion-type dog."

Jake looked at the vast face, its muzzle pressing against his thigh. He lifted the dog's face and stared into the sad, dark eyes. "I don't think my mother would care for such a large dog."

"Ah, ain't that right? Ladies like the toy dogs, but show 'em a man's dog, and they think it'll eat up all their flowers!" He guffawed again. "They're takin' mightily to that sister of yours, though. Guess Mr. Stevens was right 'bout that."

A good many of the dogs were still vying for Vivian's affection. She smiled as one stretched its long tongue to her cheek.

"Sorry they're so eager, miss." Mr. Stoker herded the animals back behind the fence. A Scottish terrier stood with complete confidence in front of Vivian, casting his piercing eyes at her, his head leaning as if to study her.

"He looks like an old man," Vivian remarked.

"That he is, miss, a curmudgeonly one." Mr. Stoker laughed. "They're more human than dog!"

Vivian offered her gloved hand, and the animal sniffed it. "I think he's rather sweet."

"Scotties make excellent watchdogs." Stevens eyed her. "That's what you wanted, isn't it, Miss Alderdice?"

Vivian turned to Mr. Stoker. "Do you have a rope or something I could tie around his neck so he won't run away?"

"Viv, you're not serious." Jake stared at her.

Mr. Stoker looked uneasy. "I don't know as I should, miss. It weren't no joke when I said he's a curmudgeon. Scotties ain't always polite, and they can get downright mischievous when the mood strikes 'em."

"If I wanted a polite dog, I would get one," said Vivian. "I rather like an animal with a mind of its own." The dog gave a deep bark, his small tail wagging.

Stevens grinned. "What will you name him, Miss Alderdice?"

Vivian examined the dog's black coat, rubbing the beard under his chin. "Pan is his name."

"Pan frolicking in the wild." Jake smiled. "How fitting."

Roger, too, had decided on the spaniel. His jumpy mood was

gone. "Let's go, Harland," he said. "If Miss Alderdice is ready." He bowed to her.

"I'm not ready," said the redhead. He leaned against the fence with one arm. Jake could see nothing but abandoned pieces of metal and one lone tree. Then, he realized a small pit bull pup lounged underneath it, its skull-shaped face dewy, and its eyes glistened with newness.

"Last of the litter, Mr. Stevens," Mr. Stoker said. "Friend of mine give him to me. That pup's got a pedigree that ain't nothin' to be ashamed of. His father was one of the finest hunting dogs I ever saw. Wrestled an eagle to the ground once."

"Did he?" Stevens eyes became intense.

"I know he looks kinda puny right now," the man continued. "But with proper training, them pit bulls are somethin' else."

"I can train him properly." Stevens' hand dropped as he looked at Mr. Stoker.

"Aren't they dangerous?" Vivian asked.

"No dog is dangerous unless his master makes him so," said the redhead.

Roger, holding on to the spaniel, cried, "For God's sake, Harland, you don't need him!"

Stevens' eyes were malicious as they examined the spaniel playing with the end of the rope hanging around its neck. "If you don't have the courage to take him, Roger, I do." The young man recoiled, holding the dog closer to him.

As they drove home in the wagon in silence, both the spaniel and terrier fell asleep. The bull pup remained alert, its beige-colored eyes fixed upon Stevens. A few times, Jake thought he saw the corner of its mouth quake.

CHAPTER 16

That same night, Jake dreamed of the pit bull puppy. In a room full of bright lights, the dog was trying to find its way out, its tongue lolled in the corner of its mouth. The lights kept flashing, and the dog could not free itself from their glare. Jake felt its gaze searing through his, begging for help.

He woke up, his neck and chest damp. He could not understand why the dream had been so frightening to him. Stevens had brought the pup down with him to dinner, introducing it as Maestro, and chuckling about how the dog already mastered the art of charming people with its bashful eyes. The animal had been shy but not unfriendly.

For the next several days, Stevens sought him out. They found quiet places in the hotel to talk. Jake was aware of how much he revealed about himself in response to Stevens' probing questions. Yet, when he asked the questions, the redhead was vague.

One evening before dinner, Jake had retired to the empty courtyard with the evening paper when Stevens stepped out with the bulldog pup. Maestro rushed forward in a peel of high-pitched squeals. He caught up to Jake and dug his claws into Jake's outstretched leg, gazing at him with his enormous eyes. As

Jake bent down to pet the animal, Stevens' pale hand pulled the animal back. "Maestro." The tone was low and dangerous and the dog retreated. "I never took you to be one who was interested in current events," the redhead remarked.

"I've just been reading about your Colonel Roosevelt." Jake turned the newspaper over so he could see the headline: THE FEARFUL CONDITION OF THE SANTIAGO ARMY.

Stevens shook his head. "Poor devils."

"Roosevelt stated the case eloquently," Jake said. "If they have a campaign planned in Havana for the fall, it wouldn't be much good to lose men to malaria and yellow fever."

"He's watching out for his comrades." The redhead nodded. "A man of integrity."

"In war, anyway," Jake murmured.

"In life too, friend.," Stevens growled. An elderly couple passing by glanced at them with bristling eyes, but the redhead seemed not to notice. "I'm about to take Maestro for a little exercise before dinner. Join us?"

"The breeze is pleasant," Jake admitted.

They walked to the wax wood forest. Whenever the dog wanted to stop and sniff at some unfamiliar shrub or bush, Stevens pulled him along and Maestro rushed to catch up with his master, yowling and whimpering.

"How is Roger fairing with the spaniel?" Jake asked.

The question seemed to annoy Stevens. "It was what I expected."

"Meaning?"

"He played with him for a day or two, he and his friends. Then he said the dog was tedious, so he had John — his valet — take the dog to Neart Castle."

"He wanted a dog for play," Jake pointed out.

Stevens let Maestro sniff at a few plants "Roger is as ornery as a devil sometimes. No courage in him."

"I gather those competitive sports he's so fond of require quite a lot of courage," Jake pointed out.

Stevens snorted "I didn't mean that kind of courage, friend."

The wind shook the rain left by the afternoon's summer storm down from the trees. Jake produced a handkerchief from his breast pocket and wiped the large drops from his face as the pup darted away from them.

Stevens looked down at the dog, "You must learn to like water, Maestro. A coddled dog is a useless dog. Fear becomes its master."

"Is a puppy not allowed to be afraid?" Jake looked straight at the redhead.

Stevens twisted the leash around his wrist. "Boys who shun fear become courageous men."

"We weren't talking about boys," Jake snapped. "We were talking about dogs."

"So we were." The redhead chuckled. "I've found little difference between them."

"You learned to shun fear as a boy, I assume?"

Stevens smiled. "'Fear creates danger, and courage dispels it.'"

"Is that Roosevelt speaking?" Jake asked warily.

"No friend," said the redhead. "Thoreau."

The redhead smiled. "When a man has that, you may rest assured he will get on in life."

"What about Roger?" Jake asked. "You don't consider him particularly courageous, yet he seems to be getting on quite well."

"Roger's bravery is merely physical," said the redhead. "But moral courage is entirely different."

They waited while the pup examined a carpet of clover. "Roosevelt and Thoreau," Jake mused. "You have strange tastes, Stevens."

"They both had the courage I speak of."

"Moral courage, you mean," Jake said.

"Each man has the courage to live life as he sees fit," said the redhead.

"I wonder if I'll ever have that courage," Jake murmured.

Stevens yanked Maestro to his feet. "You're young and studious, and you know your place."

"Is that the formula for success?" Jake asked in a rueful voice.

"A young man's future is not a scientific experiment." The man looked at him with the intense eyes. "I hope you don't treat it as such."

Jake picked up a rock and threw it into the trees. "I've watched you, Stevens. You have people's respect."

"I have that privilege," said the man in a soft tone.

"My grandfather had respect but no moral courage," said Jake, his voice shaking. "I don't want the same fate."

"And how shall you avoid it?" inquired the redhead.

"Earn my respect through dignity, virtue and honor," Jake said. "Not fear and ruthlessness like my grandfather." Maestro looked at him with somber eyes just the pit bull in his dreams had.

"I can help you, friend," said Stevens in a low tone.

Jake rose. "I count on you to do that."

They entered a thick part of the wax woods. Salamanders slither up the knotted limbs. Some slipped down but clamped their finger-like legs on the base and tried again.

"Persistent little devils," Jake remarked with a smile.

"Maestro will simply have to be more persistent, then." A salamander crawled into the shrubs. The pup fidgeted, scraping his paws on the ground.

"Maestro."

The dog looked at its master, shivering. "We ought to be getting back," he ventured.

"Not yet." The lines on Stevens' forehead grew heavy. "Maestro!"

The dog fluttered toward the shrubs, grinding its teeth in a startling growl. Stevens let go of the leash and the pup disappeared into the bushes.

"You ought to take a dog," Stevens said. "A small dog your mother wouldn't object to like a foxhound."

"I don't need a dog to teach me courage," Jake snapped.

"I wasn't suggesting you did, friend."

A squeal came through the bushes, and Maestro shot out, the salamander clinging to his hind leg. The dog kept throwing out its leg in an attempt to get rid of the creature. Jake dropped to his knees and untangled the salamander from the pup's limb. He stroked Maestro's head, murmuring comforting words. The animal gazed at its master with anxious eyes. The redhead's handsome features grew stony, and the leering smile on his lips betrayed his rage. He put his hand on the pup's head and murmured, "Too bad, Maestro."

As they made their way back to the beach in the falling sunlight, Jake suddenly became alarmed. "You're not going to punish him, are you?"

Stevens gave him an odd smile, one that made Jake's hands feel cold. "One need not always punish a dog to gain obedience."

The remark made Jake shiver.

As they entered the lobby, the redhead said, "I'm taking Roger and his friends out tonight for a little light entertainment. You'll join us?" Jake nodded.

When Jake took his place next to Vivian at dinner, he saw Stevens residing as usual at the head of the table in silence. The pup was not with him.

CHAPTER 17

After dinner, Jake waited for Stevens in the lobby. He watched people as they emerged from the dining room. Their lavish evening dress made soft sounds that echoed in the polished room. As he listened to an elderly man near him lamenting of too much sun and poor digestion, he took a few steps toward the elevator, thinking of the soothing silence in his room. Just then, the college boys emerged with Stevens at their heels.

The redhead greeted him. "Roger wants to go to the Juno."

"What's that?" asked Ivan Morvell, a young man with spectacles whose hat always seemed to be falling over his eyes.

"A variety house," said the young man. He looked seedy, as if he hadn't slept well the night before.

"I heard The Juno has fan dancers and ladies who dress as gentlemen." Willard Adams let out a spitting laugh.

"If my mother found out—" Mr. Harrington gasped.

"It ain't in this hayseed town, surely," said Mr. McDonaugh.

"Naturally not," Roger snorted. "Waxwood is much too precious for that sort of thing."

"But is it respectable, Mr. Stevens?" Mr. Harrington asked with anxious eyes.

"As respectable as such an establishment can be," said Stevens. "Mr. Shelley will help you get a wagon. We shall meet you there."

"We?" Roger gave him a sharp look.

"Jake and I will take the Brata." Stevens waved them away. The young men headed toward the ferry. Roger lingered, giving Jake a look with his razor-sharp eyes.

"The Brata?" Jake asked.

The man grinned. "My automobile."

Jake studied him. "You're an odd one, Stevens."

"Eh?"

"You go on and on about their lack of moral courage, yet you take them to a burlesque show."

"I'm not taking them, friend," the man insisted. "Roger is. You and I are coming along to make sure they don't get into mischief."

"You don't deny there is a contradiction."

"There are ways to enjoy the pleasures of life," Stevens murmured.

"Women in bloomers and short skirts don't quite fall under the category of decent men's pleasures," Jake murmured.

Stevens laughed. "I thought that Bible of yours teaches you that you must sin to be saved."

"Are you trying to save us?" Jake asked.

"Perhaps." The redhead became grave again.

Mr. Shelley was again talkative as he searched for the key to Stevens' car, and Jake feared Roger and his friends would reach Goldspur well before they did. The redhead led Jake to an automobile waiting patiently on the straw floor. "I had it custom-built." He polished the headlight with his handkerchief. "You ought to consider keeping one in the city. It won't be long before every man who is any man has one."

The car was tall and box-like, reminding him of a stately carriage. The paint shone bright red with gleaming gold scrolls and gold handles. The plush interior revealed a narrow seat and a gold-plated tiller.

The automobile hummed pleasantly, moving slow and odorless down the road. Stevens steered the car with expert ease.

"I thought these new contraptions were as clamorous as the devil," Jake remarked.

"It runs on electricity," the man said. "Silent as a deer in the woods."

The wispy wind from the coast subsided, and a calm breeze set in. Soon the car slid onto the main street of Goldspur. Jake had heard the town resembled the Barbary Coast, with its flooding gaslights and the drab and dirty streets. The scent of whiskey and beer filled the air.

"Don't get the wrong impression." Stevens watched him from the corner of his eye. "The reformers already have their eye on it, and I expect we'll see the salons and the pleasure houses disappear within the next few years. " He eased the Brata near a vacant lot.

"Aren't you afraid someone will steal it?" Jake asked.

"These people aren't dangerous," Stevens insisted. "Only poor." He glanced at a man standing nearby. The redhead tossed him some coins and the man caught them with a wink. "He'll raise his knife to anyone who comes near the Brata."

"Every man has his price?" Jake was unable to keep the distaste out of his voice.

Stevens looked at him with surprise. "Naturally, friend."

To Jake's relief, The Juno looked less run down than some of the other establishments they passed. The college boys were already ogling the posters on the walls.

Stevens' shrewd eyes regarded Jake's flushed countenance with amusement. "Have you ever been to a burlesque house?"

"Certainly," Jake snapped. It was not a lie. On several occasions, he had joined the young men of Washington Street on their excursions to the Barbary Coast where the atmosphere reeked of sawdust and perspiration and the ladies were generous with their lipstick and kisses. But unlike them, he had always felt a little sorry for the ladies and had tipped them generously.

The other young men appeared as tentative as he, except for Roger. The young man went around sporting the assured smirk of a man of the world. As they made their way through a dark hallway, they passed a few women in costume with heavily painted faces, their eyes shining like raccoons in the night. One of them, wearing a top hat and a starched shirt tucked inside a skirt cut to the edge of her thigh, grinned and saluted Stevens.

Inside the theater, the air was cool and lined with wooden benches that took advantage of every available space. The college boys wrestled with seats in the second row. Stevens chose two seats at the end of the row above.

As Jake watched the redhead's acute eyes observe the college boys settling in, he remembered the haunting words of his grandfather: *They're watching you, and they are judging!* He realized Stevens was now like those invisible eyes. The young men fidgeted, drummed their fingers against their knees, and shook out the program with more vigor than necessary. "They're nervous like little boys at a fancy party for the first time," he murmured.

The redhead let out a roaring laugh that made a few men glance at him. "You're more gullible than I thought."

"You don't believe it, then?"

"I know young men," said Stevens.

"You're a cruel judge, Stevens."

A woman with a head of dark curls, red tights and a short silk suit came fluttering down the aisle and pounced on Stevens. Jake stared in awe as she took the man's face in both her hands and gave him an enthusiastic peck on the cheek.

"Missed you, honey," she said in a sweet voice. "Thinkin' 'bout you all the time."

"Well, don't!" Stevens growled.

The girl's face crumpled like a used handkerchief, and he felt as sorry for her as he had the ladies he had met at the Barbary Coast. He spoke politely to her, introducing himself with a bow. The tears that had threatened to come from her lovely eyes disappeared, and she gave him a shy smile, then glared at the redhead as she retreated toward the back of the theater.

"You needn't have been so savage." Jake sat down again.

Stevens said in a light voice, "Tomorrow I'll send her the largest bouquet she's probably ever received in her life."

Jake forgot his anger as the show began. His attention was averted to the lively jokes and prancing figures on the stage. The college boys were genuinely in awe of the whole thing. Mr. Morvell's eyeglasses slipped down his nose, and Mr. Trent's fighting spirit elapsed into shyness as he wrung his program in his hands. Even the cool Mr. McDonaugh was biting his nails, leaned back into the seat. Only Roger seemed bored.

A woman whose skirt was shorter and less elegant than her predecessors' appeared on stage toting behind her a row of poodles riding unicycles while the crowd clapped with vigor. The young men's eyes were not on the dogs but their trainer, watching her kick her leg up with every applause. They appeared confused and uncomfortable. Jake wondered how many minstrel shows, variety acts, and burlesque houses Roger had seen. The young man's eye lingered on the woman's thighs, as she wore no stockings, but without the wonderment or appreciation of his comrades'.

Stevens' face had softened a little as he observed the college boys with their fidgeting and coughing. "You were right. They are like little boys at a fancy party."

A woman screamed. Standing on the platform was the young woman Jake had seen earlier with the top hat and starched shirt. One of the tails on her jacket was torn, and she was trying to cover her leg with the other. Her face showed the terror of a hunted animal. Roger was leaning over the empty chair in front of him, a devilish smile playing on his lips. People were glaring at him, while his friends looked on in fear. The young man laughed as his hand yanked the other tail on the woman's jacket.

Jake lunged forward and caught him by the wrist. Roger whirled around, snapping his fist in Jake's face. Jake felt the blow and stumbled backward. There were more screams, and a rotund man with a thick mustache appeared grabbing his shoulder. The college boys rushed up the aisle, and Stevens pulled Roger away by the neck.

Outside, the street look bright the scent of decayed food and tar overpowering. Stevens grabbed his cousin by the shirt collar and threw him against a poster displaying the dancer he had just insulted. Roger collapsed on the ground, his friends chuckling. He stared at Stevens with defiance.

"You're lucky we're kin, Roger." The redhead's voice was as low and dangerous as it had been with Maestro in the woods. "Damn lucky. Now get the blazes out of here!"

The young men were all looking at their friend. Roger glared at Stevens for a few moments, then rose and walked toward the alley. The college boys followed close behind, none of them daring to look back. A few moments later, the wagon came flying out with Roger cracking the whip.

Jake tried to keep up with Stevens' angry stride. The Brata was, as the redhead promised, still faithfully guarded under the leery eye of the man with the low hat and dirty boots. "Like to drive it?" The man's voice was sober, the fire in his eyes dim.

"I don't know how."

"You must learn sometime," said Stevens. "I told you, the automobile isn't going away."

Jake shook his head. The redhead stared at him, then got in and started the car.

They made their way back to Waxwood, the scent of a citrus filtering through the windows. Jake looked out at the black road, lit only by a glare from the car's headlights. "I'm sorry he was so crude, Stevens."

"Filth!" the redhead spat it out. "Roger used to be a good boy. Now he's as rotten as his father."

"He lost his head," Jake said in a soft voice.

"Don't tell me you have sympathy for him!" The man's voice grew icy. "He despises you, you know."

"I know," said Jake.

"My father took him in when he had no one," said Stevens. "Gave him the education of a gentleman. And this is how he repays him."

"What do you propose to do?" Jake asked.

The redhead's eyes arched forward. "We shall see."

The look on his face made Jake shudder, as it was the same gaze he had observed when Stevens looked down at Maestro, shivering from the encounter with the salamander.

CHAPTER 18

The next night, Jake accompanied Stevens to the York. The summer crowd was already diminishing, and the hotels showed signs of less clutter and chaos, lending a more pleasant air to the place. The cigar and cigarette smoke in the men's lounge was less congested, and the open windows let in a refreshing sea breeze.

The college boys were intent over a game of billiards. Jake absently picked up a sheet of York stationary someone had left on the table and began sketching. He became lost in the drawing until he heard Stevens' mild voice. "Well done." Jake looked up, startled. "You've drawn my cousin as he really is."

"I wasn't aware I was drawing him," Jake insisted. The redhead's mood that evening made him as jumpy as his high-strung dog.

"You asked me once if I were a mind reader." The man's smile held a touch of deviousness. "Now I'll tell you. Ancestors of mine were mesmerizers. Do you know how they did it?" Jake shook his head. "They transmitted ideas into the heads of their victims. That is the true talent of the spiritualist."

"It sounds reprehensible," Jake said.

He chuckled. "I wonder what Culver would say if he saw your work now. Rather less innocent than Diana with her crown of thorns." He lit a cigar. Roger shot across the room and held out his hand.

"You have the most atrocious manners," his cousin said. "Our Uncle Victor used to say teaching Roger to be a gentleman was like teaching a cow not to defecate in the field."

"That popinjay," the young man growled.

Stevens glanced at Jake. "Roger once had visions of becoming a Shakespearian actor rather than an architect."

"Be still, Harland."

"He recites soliloquies in front of a mirror when he's alone." He flicked his head. "The maids have heard you, you know."

"I said be still!"

"His favorite is Shylock and Iago." The redhead continued. "'A free and open nature/That thinks men honest that but seem to be so/And will as tenderly be led by th' nose/As *asses* are.'" This made the college boys laugh.

Roger gazed at him with his beaded eyes. "'Hell and night/Must bring this monstrous birth to the world's light.'"

"That's precisely Jake's portrait of you." Stevens took the sketchbook out of his hands and held it up to the young man.

Jake couldn't look at Roger nor the other boys. The air became thick with gray smoke. All the lights dimmed.

"What is it?" Roger's voice shook with curiosity.

"The amarok," the redhead said. "An Eskimo legend. A man's body with the head of a giant wolf. Rather resembles you, Roger, with those glowing eyes and sharp claws."

"Your cousin is wrong," Jake insisted. "I had no one specific in mind."

"I find it very apt," Stevens said. "A monstrous birth, just as you said. A diabolical creature of the night, the amarok."His eyes glowered.

A murmur swept through the room as Roger leaned against the table, his face distorted with repugnance. He spoke in a voice of restraint. "That's just the sort of joke you would play on me, Harland. But I'm immune to your barbarous sense of humor."

"The truth is a joke to you." Stevens gave the drawing back to Jake.

"No, Harland. The truth is a joke to *you*."

"It's hardly a joke." Stevens said. "The amarok attacks lone hunters at night. A beast of prey."

Roger set his eyes on Jake's drawing again. "Perhaps you ought to pursue an artistic profession after all."

"I'll never paint again," Jake said.

The college boys returned to their game. Roger remained, regarding Jake with sympathy. "Why?"

"Jake owes you no explanation," said his cousin.

"I didn't ask you!"

Jake played with the edge of the pencil stub. "I was told I would never be a success. Does that satisfy you?"

The young man's face turned grave. "I'm sorry to hear that, Jake."

"Don't feign regret, Roger," said his cousin. "You never felt anything for anyone in your life but yourself."

"My experience may be more limited than yours, Harland," observed the young man, "but I have one thing you haven't. Genuine empathy." He stumbled to the liquor table and poured himself a brandy.

Jake said in a quiet voice, "I begin to understand now. It's not loathing you feel for him but disappointment."

Stevens stared into the darkness that had befallen the room, puffing on his cigar.

The young men now gathered around Roger refreshing themselves on their powerful cocktails. Roger's head was bent, staring into his glass with vacant eyes. Jake approached and held out the drawing to him. "You may keep it if you wish."

Roger took the drawing, folding it carefully inside his pocket. Jake returned to his place beside Stevens.

CHAPTER 19

The sky grew black, and the sea calmed. The young men played and drank into the night, and Stevens showed no signs of retiring. Jake wanted to leave, but his feet felt cemented int hat room. He listened as their talk moved from college professors and sports to the war in Cuba.

"We ought to pull out while we can," said Mr. Harrington. "It's not worth the lives we've already given for it."

"We're not there for fancy, boy." Mr. Trent shot two balls in the left side pocket. "Let Spain and every other country see we're a force to be reckoned with."

Mr. McDonaugh cocked his head. "The frontier's all taken, so what have we left?"

"Virile man conquer virgin territory," Roger agreed, his words sounding thick.

"We've almost won anyway," said Ivan Morvell. "Not two weeks ago, the Rough Riders—"

"Those braggarts!" Roger snarled. "Posing for the papers like gladiators. And that goose with his mustache and spectacles!"

Stevens jumped up. In the shadow left by two lamp, his indignation was unavoidable. "I suggest you speak about Mr. Roosevelt with respect."

"They did all right on Kettle Hill," Mr. Trent insisted. "Them and those Buffalo Soldiers."

"They have grit, to be sure," the young man admitted. "But it won't last, not with that asthmatic runt at the helm."

"You're an ass, Roger." Stevens' thundering voice made the room shudder.

"We're just talking, Mr. Stevens." Mr. Harrigan twitched.

"Mr. Roosevelt is a man of our time," the redhead declared. "A real man of our time."

Roger turned to Jake. "Are you also an admirer of the great Teddy Roosevelt?"

"I know only what I read in the papers," Jake murmured.

"Mr. Roosevelt is a great one for the papers." The young man's stick dropped, and he had some trouble retrieving it.

"You're drunk, Roger," said Stevens. "The words of a drunkard are the words of a fool."

"You ought to hear Harland on the subject of Roosevelt," his cousin continued. "You would think he was Hercules and Lincoln rolled into one. Praise be, the man's man has arrived at last!" He waved his arms.

"I think we need some air," said Mr. McDonaugh. "How about it?" He reached for his friend's arm, but the man shoved him away.

"Why don't we all get some air?" Stevens suggested.

The others looked at the two men with fear and wonderment. Roger gave a convulsive laugh and stumbled out the door. His friends followed.

The redhead grinned at Jake. "Shall we enjoy the night air?"

"I think I'll go to bed."

"Nonsense," said Stevens. "It's the perfect time for a walk on the beach."

"Leave him alone, Stevens." Jake begged.

"I won't say a word," said the man. "Coming?"

They found the young men to the boardwalk as they howled like cowboys, galloping over a rainbow of flowers outside the York. Stevens bent over a cluster of jasmine smashed by the exuberant feet. Jake watched with amazement as the man cradled them in his hands. "My mother keeps a garden at the castle." He tried to turn the petals upright, but they flopped over in grief. "Odd such delicate flowers should bloom in this sea air, isn't it?" He looked at Jake with a soft smile. "Nature is more resilient than we think."

"More resilient than we are." Jake nodded in agreement.

The redhead gazed at the college boys who had gone down to the beach with cold fury.

Willard Adams produced a handful of cigars from his coat pocket and passed them around. The raw scent of the sea folded inside the harsh smoke, tripping along the beach like children in search of their mothers. Roger fell face first into the sand. He rolled over, looking befuddled at the smashed cigar in his mouth. Mr. Trent howled, holding his knees as he laughed like a clown. Roger leapt up and threw him down with a savagery that could only come from a drunken rage. "You lily-livered pigeon!"

"Lily-livered!" Mr. Trent's voice ripped through the dim beach.

Jake glanced at Stevens, but the redhead only looked on with some interest. Jake took a few steps forward, but Mr. Trent's temper deflated, and he rose, brushing sand from his shirt.

"My father taught me never to strike a man who can't hold his liquor." He ran down the beach, his legs surprisingly nimble given his state of intoxication. Roger and the others staggered after him.

"Why didn't you stop them?" Jake hissed.

"Nothing happened," the redhead said coolly.

"That man might be carrying a gun!"

Stevens cast an amused eye upon him. "A wise man must first be a fool."

"This was more than tomfoolery!" Jake exploded. "He might have killed your cousin!"

"He would have been well within his rights." Stevens sounded almost philosophical. "Roger accused him of being a coward."

Jake's blood ran cold. "You talk as if you wish he had drawn a pistol."

"If it would have come to that, I would have gone for it," said the redhead. "I have some family feeling."

Jake looked at him with scorn. "He's disappointed you, so now you're getting even."

The redhead looked at him with amusement. "I don't intend to leave them to their own devices for long, if that reassures you." He followed the young men's slow-moving figures in the distance.

Jake rushed after him. "Are you really that disgusted with their infantine pursuits? Or is it because they're still young enough to have them?"

The man grabbed Jake's wrist, twisting it hard. Panic seized Jake as he tried to wrench free. The man let go and gave him a capturing smile. "My apologies."

Jake mumbled, "I didn't mean what I said."

"Naturally not," said the redhead. "We're all a little tight tonight, aren't we?"

They found the college boys near one of the smaller hotels. Lights were strung all along the empty veranda, the swinging lanterns brightened the dark waters.

"The ghost ship!" Mr. Harrington's eyes and mouth opened, his usual exasperation coupled with fear.

Jake's studied the mast flaring up like the arms of a beautiful woman. The railing looked rusty and was missing in some places. The sails were torn and one of the three chimneys tilted toward the water. Yet he could still feel the seductive power of the nautical monster.

"One magnificent giant, isn't it?" Stevens murmured.

Roger hurled a whiskey bottle against the side of the ship. The shattering noise brought about an eerie scream from a far-away bird.

"How dare you show such disrespect for this fine beast!" His cousin growled.

"Your fine beast looks ready to collapse," Roger scoffed.

"This iron giant will survive far longer than any of its observers."

"Giants wrangle their prey, don't they?" Jake remembered the line from his great-grandfather's book.

"Unless their prey wrangles them first," Stevens said. "Why don't you, Roger."

The young man stared at his cousin. "What the devil do you mean?"

"You and Jake," said Stevens. "A game of courage, if you please."

"A game of clods, you mean," Roger snapped. "It wouldn't be safe for even a seagull to land on that deck."

Stevens grinned. "It would be a magnificent adventure. Conquering the Trojan horse." The man threw back his head and laughed. "Or is it you and not your friend who is the coward?"

"I won't do it!" Then, in a more appeasing tone, he added, "Don't do it, Jake. He's playing with us just as he plays with his dogs." There was genuine fear in his voice. "What he does to those dogs—"

"You're the one who's playing, Roger." The redhead's voice thundered in the dark, "Playing at being a man."

"I said I wouldn't do it and I won't," said his cousin. "What Jake does is his own business."

"Did you hear that, Jake?" he asked. "Like the knights of old, Roger has just thrown down the gauntlet."

"I did no such thing, and you know it!"

Stevens said to Jake in a low voice, "You're not going to let that challenge go, are you?"

Jake looked at the rusted ghost. The young men stared at him in silence.

"Don't do it!" Roger howled.

"He's afraid," Stevens whispered. "He knows if you climb the beast, he must do it as well."

"He's drunk, Stevens."

"My cousin has more physical prowess drunk than sober," the redhead insisted.

"I don't know—"

"*I* know," the man hissed. "I have faith in you."

The excitement in the redhead's face touched Jake. His grandfather had never said such a thing to him. He slipped off his jacket and threw it into the sand.

"Fool!" Roger screamed.

The moment Jake stepped on the deck, he saw Stevens was right. He had indeed embarked on a magnificent adventure. Mist touched his shoulders, and moonlight stroked his cheek. Wind rang through the ship's fluted passages, the deck vibrating under his feet. His heart beat faster. The nautical monster came to life, swaying to *his* rhythm.

Shouts below that brought him out of his reverie. Looking down into the swirling black sea, he saw a man rising from the water, his eyes fiendishly plated gold. The image disappeared as he found himself on dry land.

"Well done!" Stevens handed him his coat. "The conquering hero. You shall climb to great heights, Jake."

The college boys surrounded him, their heads blocking the moonlight, their hands gruffly shaking his, hailing good wishes in shaking voices.

When he rose, he saw Roger ascending the gangplank. The young man's gait was unsteady, his hips swaying dangerously, yet he kept at it. But just shy of the deck, he lost his balance and jumped from the gangplank into the shallow water.

A burst of laughter reached Jake's ears. His temper burst forward. "You laugh while your friend may be hurt!"

He ran toward the sea, helping the young man to safety. Roger tore away from him into the net of friends who had sobered enough to court remorse for their behavior. "This finishes us, Harland." He looked at Stevens as if at a stranger.

The redhead began walking back toward the boardwalk. Jake silently followed, looking back only once. Roger and his friends disappeared from view. Only the ship stood in the glimmering moonlight.

CHAPTER 20

"Your Mr. Stevens seems to have chased Roger and his friends away." Vivian remarked the next evening at cocktails. Stevens sat alone looking at the sea with Maestro dozing at his feet.

"Huey was saying this morning he saw them taking the ferry into town," Larissa observed.

The cocktail tasted bitter on Jake's lips.

"I would think those young wolves would be beneath his notice." Marvina, who had joined them, chuckled.

His mother folded the letter she had been reading back in its envelope. "They would be, except he thought it odd they had their baggage with them."

"Did they?" Vivian sat up.

"I'm sure he was mistaken," Jake said hurriedly.

"Why don't we ask their chaperone?" Before he could stop her, Vivian made a motion with her hand. The redhead immediately rose.

"An evening like this makes one feel like a child again, doesn't it?" Jake noticed an underlying turbulence under Stevens' usual mild manner.

"We used to sit outside on evenings like this, and Viv would make me a crown out of flowers." He was aware his voice sounded spasmodic in the serene summer air.

"What a charming idea," Stevens said. "I would like a crown like that one day."

"Perhaps I shall weave you a crown of thorns instead, Mr. Stevens," Vivian said.

"If you do," he said with sparkling eyes, "I shall reward you with a bow and arrow." He turned to Larissa, explaining, "Jake painted his sister was like Diana, the Grecian wood nymph. I don't think Miss Alderdice appreciates the comparison, though."

"On the contrary, Mr. Stevens," said Vivian, "I rather admire Diana. She turned a man into a stag so his own hunting dogs would eat him alive."

"She had good reason," Stevens said. "Actaeon violated her chastity. If one has committed a crime or a sin, one must pay for it."

"There are equal crimes and sins that are not against women," Vivian said. "I noticed that dog of yours looks a little weak." She glanced down at Maestro who indeed looked as if he had fallen among the daffodils languishing on the plot beside their table.

"I'm afraid I've been neglecting his exercise." He patted the dog's head.

"Perhaps you and I may walk both our dogs one morning," he said. "Scottish terriers are rather active."

"And rather loud," Larissa said ruefully.

"Mother made me send Pan back to the city."

"Oh?" The man's eyebrows raised.

"I had no objections," Vivian continued. "Mother was right. His barking was rather loud. He was flustered with all these people about."

"It wasn't the people, dear," said her mother. "You were spoiling him too much."

"A coddled dog is a useless dog," Jake quoted, making Stevens smile.

"The poor thing was so miserable here," Vivian insisted. "I think Maestro is miserable too." She regarded the pup with pitying eyes. The dog returned her look with a wide, damp stare.

"He does look rather dismal," Marvina admitted.

"I wonder why that is, Mr. Stevens," his sister said.

"Don't insinuate, Viv," Jake growled.

The redhead leaned back in his chair. "Perhaps because I had to break some of his obstinate will."

"As with boys, so is it with dogs?" Vivian eyed him.

"Vivian!" Larissa's warning voice shot above the light chatter.

"My brother accused me of insinuating," Vivian said. "So I'll be direct, Mr. Stevens. Why did you banish your cousin and his friends?"

Stevens was quiet for a moment. "I haven't banished them, Miss Alderdice. They left of their own accord."

"I apologize for my daughter's forthrightness," Larissa glared at her.

"I've a feeling Mr. Stevens finds it refreshing," said Marivina, leaning back with a smile.

The man's smile froze as he picked up the cocktail glass and drank it down. "Perhaps I do."

"Your perseverance with their education speaks to your good will, Mr. Stevens," said Larissa.

"It's a shame that education did not extend to their behavior," Vivian murmured.

"One cannot force a lion to be a lamb," her mother snapped.

"Quite right," Jake said.

"So you took it upon yourself to try and teach those young men manners?" Marvina asked. "That was a noble experiment."

"If you didn't banish them, then why did they leave?" asked Vivian.

"They were bored." Jake felt his anger rising as well. "Don't make a mystery of it, Viv."

"They didn't seem bored," his sister pointed out. "I always saw them having a good time."

He set his glass down with a clatter. "They were climbing the walls trying to find what to do with themselves. Isn't that so, Stevens?"

Stevens stared down at Maestro playing with a butterfly in the grass. "Since you persist in knowing, Miss Alderdice, I shall tell you exactly why my cousin left. Your brother is being discreet when he says Roger was bored but, as you say, that isn't the reason." He picked up the dog and settled him in his lap. "He embarrassed himself last night to the point where there was nothing else for him to do but leave."

"Did he?" She looked at him with interest. "What did he do that was so reprehensible?"

The redhead gave her a fiendish look. "Roger challenged your brother. He lost the challenge."

"What sort of challenge?" Larissa's figure was at once alert with maternal concern.

"It wasn't anything, Mother," Jake assured her.

"Roger had a notion to board that ship in the shallow waters," said the redhead. "Jake managed it. My cousin didn't get past the gang plank."

Jake bit his lip. "It wasn't dangerous, Mother."

"It was a childish thing to do, Jacob."

"He didn't have much choice, ma'am." The redhead played with his glass. "His peers would have reproached him if he hadn't done it."

"That's the most idiotic thing I've ever heard!" Vivian exploded.

Stevens gave her a wary look. "I didn't think you would approve, Miss Alderdice."

"I suppose it was foolish," Marvina said with a sigh. "But young men must do foolish things to become wise men."

"Very well put, Mrs. Moore." Stevens smiled. "I would have made sure not one of them came to any harm." He motioned for the waiter. Jake felt a little uneasy as he realized it was the redhead's third cocktail. "My father taught me never to turn down a challenge, no matter how foolish, if I knew I could win."

"Was your father such a tyrant?"

"Vivian!" his mother snapped.

Stevens extracted a pocket lighter from his pocket and held it in his hand, twisting it between his fingers upside down and then right side up. "Perhaps one day you shall meet him and judge for yourself."

"My husband and I met your father some years ago," said Mrs. Moore. "I recall he was quite affable."

"Thank you for saying so, ma'am." Stevens gave her a quick bow.

"Perhaps Roger was taught differently," said Vivian. "*He* seemed quite affable to me."

"My father guided him," said the redhead. "Roger's was a weak-willed man, I'm afraid."

Jake thought of the young man who, only the night before, had shown empathy toward him. "You're not being very kind toward your uncle," he mumbled.

"I don't blame him," said Stevens. "He came back from the Civil War a broken man."

"So your father took it upon himself to be his guide in the art of brutality?" Vivian eyed him. "How very noble."

Stevens gave her a cool stare. "Your forthrightness is brutal, Miss Alderdice."

"And very unladylike," Larissa snapped. "Vivian, I've had enough."

"It is a little, dearest," Marvina said softly.

"You've ceased to be charming, Viv," Jake agreed.

"I don't think Mr. Stevens has ceased to be charmed." Vivian gazed at him. "I rather think he likes an unladylike lady."

The redhead chuckled. "You haven't ceased to fascinate me. That I will admit."

"Why is that?"

"You're more courageous and strong-willed than most men I've met," said the redhead. "That is something to be admired."

"Then you admire women with courage and strong will?" Marvina asked.

"Men and women," he said. "I consider those two qualities to be of the highest virtue."

"And those young men of yours had neither?" Vivian asked.

"I made no secret of my intentions toward Roger and his friends when I invited them to join me in Waxwood this summer," said Stevens. "I appreciated their youthful energy, but I was trying to redirect it."

"My father tried to do the same with young men who came to work for him," Larissa said. "Those he thought had enough presence of mind, that is."

"Most wise men do," Stevens said. "My father taught me that a man cannot progress without courage and strong will and, if you'll pardon, a little manly aggression."

The waiter came around to light the rest of the lanterns. Under the moony glow, the man's face showed softer angles. "I apologize for sermonizing," he said. "I'm very passionate about the subject of young men's education."

"It's been fascinating." Mrs. Moore pulled her shawl closer to her shoulders. "I shall think of what you have said for a long time."

"I'm happy to have enlightened you, ma'am." He bowed.

Larissa sipped at her cocktail. "I'm glad you've taken an interest in Jacob, Mr. Stevens."

"I wonder if your father would admire courage and strong will in a woman," Vivian said slyly.

The corner of the redhead's lip twitched. "That is a question indeed, Miss Alderdice."

"Perhaps I will meet him one day and find out for myself." She sat back, looking over the hedge at the sea. Jake did not miss the spark on Stevens' face.

CHAPTER 21

*I*n the morning, Stevens did not wait for the Alderdices to invite him to join them. He strolled over the moment he entered the dining room, Maestro at his heels. He greeted the ladies with his usual bow, but Jake could see something preoccupied his mind. His eyes darted absently around the dining room.

"You are not going to the picnic, Mr. Stevens?" his mother asked. "I daresay it will be one of the last of the season."

"No, ma'am," he said. "I was hoping Jake might come with me. There are some important people I think it would be worth his while to meet."

Something in the way he pronounced each word with heavy intent, as a schoolteacher providing instruction to a child, made Jake drop the orange in his hand. Maestro retrieved it like a ball.

Larissa gave Stevens her hostess smile. "Business associates of yours?"

"Yes, ma'am," the redhead mumbled

"I thought you were on vacation," Vivian said.

"One must still think of business while one is on vacation, dear," said Larissa.

"Regrettably, that's true," Stevens said. "We ought to be back by dinner, if not sooner."

Jake picked up the pit bull pup. The animal gazed at him with the look Jake remembered from that day in the woods — anxious and quivering. "I was rather looking forward to going on the picnic," he mumbled.

"It won't be as tedious as you think," Stevens said with a grin. "I promise it will be worth your time."

Larissa's voice was as steely as her gaze. "I think you should go, Jacob."

He glanced at his mother, seeing beneath the iron countenance a shadow of a plea.

The Brata had been polished since the last time Jake saw it. The redhead eyed him as they turned into the quiet road toward Goldspur. "You don't seem the least bit curious, friend."

"Should I be?" Jake asked.

The man yanked a handkerchief out of his pocket and wiped his brow. "I always am about meeting new people."

"I don't relish mysteries," Jake snapped.

"You needn't be skittish," said the redhead. "I'm introducing you to a very worthy fraternity."

"Fraternity?" Jake stared at him.

"Have you ever belonged to one?"

Jake shook his head. "My grandfather did. He made some valuable business connections there, but that was all he would tell me about it."

"Now, that's very interesting." Stevens slowed the car.

"I thought all his secrecy was all rather silly," Jake said.

"Fraternities are very serious," said the redhead. "All men should belong to at least one."

"Is that another of your rules of success?"

"No, friend," he said. "This one is personal."

They were silent for a time. Then, Jake asked, "What's their name?"

"The Order of Actaeon," said Stevens.

Jake shook his head. "I've never heard of them."

"You wouldn't," said the man. "They don't come out from behind the shadows like the Freemasons or some of the others."

"how long have you been a member of this fraternity?"

Stevens steered the car a little to the left. "Since I was your age."

Jake blinked. "I never took you for one to follow a crowd."

"They're very exclusive," he said.

"What makes you think they'll accept me even with your sponsorship?"

"Because when you climbed that ship, you showed me you had not only courage and strong will but integrity," said the redhead.

Jake winced. "Perhaps these men will find me less worthy than you."

Stevens laughed and turned the car onto a prickly dirt road. "Worth is self-made, friend, not given."

They were bumping down a path so narrow the tree limbs brushed against the window. The rumbling road echoed inside the car. Stevens eased the Brata under a circle of pines, then jumped down, his steps quickening over the ragged ground. Jake descended more slowly, feeling the trees eyeing them with suspicion.

Stevens seemed driven by instinct, his gaze searching for some invisible destination. His stride was even longer than usual, and Jake became breathless trying to keep up with him. They reached a clearing where a group of men were waiting. Some were older than Stevens and some younger than Jake. The redhead turned to Jake and spread his arms out. "Welcome to the Order of Actaeon."

"Are you mad, friend?" snarled a man with a bushy beard.

"I told you I had a new recruit," said Stevens. "You doubted me?"

"But like this, out in the open—"

"We can trust him, Smith," the redhead insisted.

"He looks gullible as a newborn babe!" Smith snorted.

"So did you when you first joined." Another man spoke with an amiable tone. "Let's hear what the young man has to say for himself."

"I've told him nothing, of course," said Stevens. He then took Smith and the amiable man aside and spoke to them in low whispers. Th other men stared at Jake, intent as lizards.

"We understand you want to join our order," said the amiable man.

"I don't know." Jake glanced at the mooning faces.

The man looked at Stevens.

The redhead leaned toward Jake, speaking in a very low voice, "You won't disappoint me like Roger, will you?"

Jake remembered Stevens' words when they drove home from The Juno, his disappointment and hurt. He remembered the beach: *I have faith in you.* "Yes, if you'll have me," he said.

"If Duff speaks highly of you, we shall have you," said the man. He gave Smith a meaningful look. The man nodded. "What name do you choose?"

"Name?"

"You must take a name by which no one in the civilized world knows you."

Jake blinked into the sunlight falling into his eyes.

The man held out his hand. "I'm Lorimar," he said. "Don't be afraid, son. You're among friends here. What name?"

"Carlyle, sir." It was his grandmother maiden name.

Lorimar presented the rest of the men. Each stepped forward to shake his hand, cautious but friendly. "And you're willing to take our oaths and abide by our principles and philosophies?"

"To answer that question, I must hear what they are first," Jake said.

The man chuckled. "A young man with caution and judgment." He nodded with approval. "To know about us is to know a little about our past." He put weight on some words more than others, and Jake wondered if he were a politician in the "civilized world."

"Yes," Jake said vaguely. "I've heard that before." One named Pines, whose fresh face made it clear he was even younger than Jake, looked at him with wide eyes.

Lorimar continued. "Smith, Allcock, and I came together to form this group some time ago. Two of us are still here." He nodded at Smith.

"And where is the third?" Jake asked.

"Allcock broke the first oath of our order." Lorimar said gravely. "No one must know about us. Secrecy is imperative. Do you swear?"

"I swear to secrecy, sir." Jake felt bolder.

"Our second oath," the man continued, "is to transpose nothing from our civilized world into the world of the order."

Smith added, "All of us have a life outside the order. We leave all that behind when we meet."

"We have no quarrel with anyone, nor do we break any laws," Lorimar said firmly. "But our philosophies are sometimes misunderstood, so we wish them to be disconnected from our civilized lives."

"Yes, I take the oath," said Jake.

"The third oath is to live in peaceful fraternity with others in the order."

"Peaceful fraternity," Jake echoed.

"Younger members such as yourself are on their path to success," said Lorimar. "We take it upon ourselves to guide them. We do not regard one another as competitors as they do in the civilized world."

"I swear to peaceful fraternity," Jake said.

The man now put his hand on Jake's shoulder. "The fourth oath is to accept whatever we have to teach you."

"Our philosophy is based on what we think modern man will be in the years to come," said Smith. "We teach that to lads like yourself."

"Mr. Roosevelt's philosophy." Jake remembered Stevens' fondness for quoting the man.

Lorimar smiled. "Duff has taught you well. Yes, we honor prowess and success, but at the same time, manly virtue and virility."

A man introduced to Jake as Cadden said, "In simple terms, lad, we prefer the teachings of pure-minded men."

"Is there such a thing?" Jake's voice echoed in the stillness.

Lorimar laughed. "You ask a wise question for one so young. And your sincerity is clearly in line with ours." He gave Stevens another approving glance. "Perhaps there is some question of purity in this day and age. We don't deny that."

"But when we come together, we follow a pure path as closely as possible," said another man with curling locks who stroked his chin, a man named Philpot.

Jake looked at Stevens. The redhead sat under a pine, examining a large pinecone in his hands as if he were not there.

"Yes, sir, I swear," he said.

"Our fifth oath is discretion amongst ourselves," Lorimar said. "We don't ask questions about one another's life outside of the order."

"I promise not to ask questions." Jake pressed his hands together.

"Then you swear allegiance to all these oaths, my boy?" Lorimar asked.

"Yes, sir!"

"Even to let go of everything that grows away from you?" Asked Smith.

Lorimar glanced at him. "That comes later. We welcome you, Carlyle, and we hope you find us as worthy as we will find you."

"He will," Stevens said, rising. "Carlyle is uncorrupted and incorruptible."

The men came forward, shaking Jake's hand, their faces relaxed and trusting.

"Stevens shall guide you," said Lorimar. "You're one of us now, my boy."

Jake's apprehension lifted, and he felt a strange fullness. He caught a glimpse of Pines. The young man's face hung with creases that seemed too old for his years.

CHAPTER 22

"Now, gentlemen," Stevens' voice rose over the lull. "I've found a solution to our problem. If you'll follow us, I will show you."

A little before the entrance to Waxwood, Stevens turned, into a steep hill with a worn road. The sight of wild violets warmed Jake, and he opened the window. The breeze was sour and icy. "Are we far away from the sea?" he asked.

"Just past the woods," Stevens answered.

The flowers disappeared into pine trees and redwoods, where Stevens stopped the car. The ground was crumbled and rocky.

The men followed them through a thicket of dense. The sun offered light, but its heat quickly dissipated as a mist encircled them. Vines lurched forward, snagging at his shirt. The place was unusually quiet without even the peep of a bird. The potential for violence seemed to lurk behind every tree.

They were walking among the wax wood trees, differed from the ones he and Vivian discovered. Their wood was smoky, and their leaves serrated like little saws. They came upon a strange-looking gate haphazardly built out of gnarled wood. Figures were carved into it, their faces staring at him with phantom eyes.

Stevens produced a key from his coat pocket and looked at Jake with warning. "You must never tell your sister about this."

"I'll keep the vow of secrecy," Jake promised.

"I didn't mean that," said the redhead. "I mean about *this*."

"Why would it interest her?" Jake asked.

The man only looked at him with apprehension as he opened the gate.

At first, it didn't look like much — a barricade of redwoods less disconcerting than the ones they had passed amidst tangled shrubs and vines. Stevens called to the other men behind them, "We'll have to clear some of this away, of course."

Jake pushed through the overgrowth and shot forward, his shoulder hitting the wall of what looked like a small, abandoned house. The roof was peaked with red tiles, whereas other houses were flat and simple. Jake peered inside the insect-stained window, staring at an empty parlor. "Another one of your ghost towns?" he murmured.

"The same one," said Stevens.

He remembered his sister's words: *Some things, once locked, ought to stay locked.*

The men reached them and stared with bewilderment.

"What is all this, Duff?" asked a man named Boswell, whose hair flamed redder than Stevens'.

"I told you," said Stevens. "A solution to our problem."

"What problem?" Jake asked.

"We need a new place for our camp," he explained. "Our old one was discovered."

"Where are we?" Pines stared at the red house.

"Have any of you ever heard of Brandywine?" Stevens glanced at the men.

"Some bohemian village, as I recollect," said Smith.

"No, sir," said the redhead. "It was a well-respected art colony some fifty years ago. Now it's at our disposal."

"Just like that?" Lorimar eyed him.

"Just like that." The redhead smiled. "I've scoured these woods. I've spotted pheasants and ducks and the other day, I saw a few deer."

"Early in the season for deer," Smith remarked.

"People were familiar with Brandywine," said Lorimar. "If some of them should get curious—"

"No one has been curious about Brandywine in five years," Stevens insisted. "It was a blemish on the town's name. Waxwood people are glad to forget."

"And the tourists?"

"Their interest is in the beach and the hotels," said the redhead. "Carlyle and I have seen that."

"A blemish," Pines said in a sad voice. "And so it didn't survive."

"We shall profit from their loss, young 'un." Smith gave him a hard pat on the back.

"And no one will run us off?" Lorimar asked.

"No one will know," promised Stevens.

The man looked at the others, who slowly gave in with silent nods. He took Stevens' hand and shook it.

As they drove back to the hotel, Jake's mind was buzzing. "Vivian gave you the idea, didn't she?"

"I don't follow you, friend." There was an edge in Stevens' voice.

"That day we went up the hill," he said. "You insisted on seeing it because you had it in mind for the Order."

"I had an idea it might suit us when she mentioned it was abandoned," the redhead admitted.

Jake was silent for a while. "Brandywine means something to Vivian."

"So she said." Stevens nodded. "'Once it had a vibrant future.' That's what gave me the idea. We have the power to make it vibrant again for our own purposes."

CHAPTER 23

As the days moved into August, he and Stevens fell into their roles dictated by the Order. The redhead waited for him every morning in the lobby after breakfast. He would give him an authoritative smile as they walked to the stables. They would drive to Brandywine where some of the men would be waiting. They spent the first week clearing the brush and vines. After that, they began what Lorimar called "building a pure existence."

Jake helped Stevens, who showed a surprisingly deft hand at carpentry. They made small furniture to fill the empty houses. They spent most of the day building, and Jake would return to the hotel with sore muscles and splintered hands, but beaming with accomplishment. Stevens was lenient with his mistakes, but some of the other older men were harsher. One day, Pines made a blunder and while no one was hurt, the enraged Smith grabbed a hammer and threw it at youth. Pines was quick to lunge away, which, Jake realized later, had been Smith's intention. The look in the young man's eyes reminded Jake of the pit bull pup waiting for the blow to fall on its head.

Later, Jake asked, "Why didn't anybody stop him?"

"A Patriarch may guide his Youth any way he sees fit," the redhead said. "Pines was careless, and Smith had the right to punish him."

"He could have seriously hurt the boy!"

Stevens gave him a meaningful glance. "He was only trying to frighten him. Pines has a dreamy nature and it distracts him. That could hurt someone one day, especially when we begin to hunt."

"When will that be?"

Stevens glanced at him. "Nervous?"

"I've never been on a hunt," Jake admitted.

The redhead grinned. "It's my duty to help you and I will."

Stevens lent him several books on hunting, and one day, he took him to a gunsmith in Goldspur and explained to him the various rifles on display. The Winchester 1897 impressed Jake.

"Why don't you buy it?"

"I haven't the money." He was ashamed to admit he would need to ask his mother for it, which he couldn't do without telling her what it was for.

The next morning, when he met Stevens in the lobby, the redhead asked, "Do you still have those paintings you showed Mr. Culver?"

"I never want to see them again," he declared.

"I didn't ask you if you wanted to see them," Stevens said. "I asked if you still have them."

Jake nodded. "In the hotel basement."

The redhead pressed Jake's shoulder. "You want that rifle, don't you? I know of a woman who would pay well for them."

Jake blinked, feeling the stinging light in his eyes. "Mr. Culver implied no one would ever want them."

"I told you, Culver embraces mendacity," said Stevens. "This woman, on the other hand, appreciates sincerity in all things, including art. Your pictures are nothing if not sincere."

"Do you really think she would like them?" His eyes lit up.

"I guarantee it, friend." The redhead grinned.

They had a time finding the man who allowed Jake to store his paintings in the basement, but at last they caught sight of him in back of the hotel having a smoke. With Stevens' promise of a box of good cigars, the man gratefully led them into the bowels of the hotel. Jake searched the shelves, his hands dampening. Stevens watched him with his eagle eye.

Jake found the shelves but when he began moving boxes aside, he knocked down a box, spilling old shoes and boots all over the floor. The redhead grasped his shoulder. "Close this chapter of your life so you can begin a new one."

Jake looked at him, feeling his eyes grow heavy.

They drove to Goldspur in meditative silence. Stevens parked, and the same man who had kept watch on the Brata when they were at The Juno emerged from the alley, giving them a sweeping bow. The redhead pressed money into his hand and grinned at Jake.

They walked past the theaters and saloons and reached a residential area. Some houses looked almost elegant, mocking picture postcards of lavish Nob Hill mansions. A few young women in white linen aprons and frosted hats passed them, heading down the incline. Jake guessed they were maids who worked in the houses.

A mansion stood at the top of the incline trimmed with gold and etched with pink angels. A sign flapped in the wind — *Juana Swivler's Fine Establishment for Gentlemen*.

Jake's face grew clammy as Stevens' eyes sparkled with amusement. "You didn't think Roger was the only one acquainted with women of fine taste and questionable morals, did you?"

Jake bit his lip. "This is — a house of ill repute."

The redhead roared, his gloved hand touching the knocker. "I should have known you would find a delicate name for it." As they waited, Stevens said, "These women are no different from those you know, except for their honest pursuit of financial advantages."

A butler led them into a small, empty parlor as fussy as Jake had ever seen in any house on Washington Street, crammed with rose-colored chairs, two settees, and bric-à-brac at every corner. Stevens produced his card, and they sat in silence as a light of roses entered the room. Jake could not hear a sound from anywhere in the house.

"Is no one at home?" He fidgeted with his hat.

"The ladies are still asleep, I imagine."

"I imagine so." Jake flipped his silk gloves over.

The redhead's face lost its amusement. "You don't approve."

"I'm perplexed," he admitted.

"Because I am well acquainted with such a place?" Stevens asked. "I told you I sowed my wild oats in my youth. I won't tell you who brought me here. The shock might be too great."

The most exquisite woman Jake had ever seen entered the room. She was not young, but her middle age wore well on her and gave her a comforting air. Sparkling combs swept up her black hair, and her dress showed the finest silk and taffeta. She was more attractive than beautiful, her figure full and lovely. "It's been so long since I've seen you, Harland." Stevens kissed both her hands and smiled with genuine affection.

"My friend, Mr. Jake Alderdice," he said. "Jake, this is Mrs. Swivler."

"Juana to all Harland's friends." Her voice was soft and melodic as she held out her hand.

"A pleasure, ma'am," said Jake, repeating Stevens' greeting.

"Marina has been asking about you," said the woman, glancing at the redhead. "She believes she's solved the riddle you gave her the last time." She set her eye on Jake. "I think your bashful friend might get along well with Geneva. You haven't met her yet."

"Not this time, Juana," said the redhead. "It's business this time."

"Oh?"

"You know I'm always looking out for your interests."

"How well I know," she said in a sly voice. "The Stevens men have been very generous."

It took Jake a few moments to realize whom "the Stevens men" were. He suspected the redhead's father had been the one who him to Juana.

"You know I don't approve of serious talk in the parlor," she said. "One ought to always conduct business in the proper atmosphere, don't you think?" She glanced at Jake, who gave a jerky nod.

"You're the most canny woman of affairs I know." A note of admiration crept into the redhead's voice.

"We shall go to my office, then." She took Stevens' arm. "Mr. Alderdice will join us?"

"I think not," said the redhead, to Jake's surprise. "This business is between you and me."

"May I suggest he retire to the main parlor, then?" Juana smiled at him. "You'll find coffee and tea with bread and butter."

"But, ma'am —"

"You'll enjoy it, I'm sure," she insisted.

"Yes, ma'am." Jake rose with a bow.

"What lovely manners you have, young man," she remarked. "It's a shame you're a dying breed these days." She looked at Stevens. "You ought to encourage that young cousin of yours not to succumb to such ruffian habits, Harland."

"Jake was brought up with the old values," said Stevens. "Roger was as well, but he ignores them."

The woman waved her fan at him. "I doubt you'll find more than a few strangling birds in the parlor at this time of day. They keep a different schedule than most people."

"Perhaps I ought to stay here, ma'am," Jake ventured. "I wouldn't want to disturb anyone."

"Well-mannered and thoughtful." She nodded with approval.

"This parlor is only for receiving, Mr. Alderdice. You shall enjoy your wait much more in the main parlor.."

"As you wish, ma'am." He bowed.

She led them through a pair of angel-carved doors, glancing back at Jake with a twinkle in her fine blue eyes. "I think this eases your discomfort."

The room was bright with pink curtains drawn back from tall windows. The furnishings were arranged cleverly to make their fussiness less noticeable. Three ladies sat fully dressed and ready for the day. They looked no different from the women of Washington Street with their silk and lace dresses and their hair lovingly piled atop their heads. Their expressions even mirrored the same diffidence, unimpressed by the visitors.

Juana introduced them by their first names. Marian, who looked to be Larissa's age, gave him a queenly nod. Becky, a scraggly woman, smiled briefly as she balanced a cup and saucer in one hand and a plate of rolls and jam in the other. Geneva was an ethereal-looking blond, so emaciated she could barely hold her cup.

With a boldness that made Jake blush, Juana declared, "Ladies, Mr. Alderdice is a visitor, not a client, so mind your manners."

The ladies relaxed, and observed Jake as he lingered near the doors through which Juana and Stevens had left. Marian invited him to sit in a comfortable chair. He politely declined, wandering to the table laid out with coffee and toast. "May I?" He smiled, gently extracting the coffeepot from Geneva's hand. It was heavy and scalding.

Marian clicked her tongue. "You ought to be in bed, dear."

"I can't stand it anymore," the girl declared in a high-pitched voice. She looked at Jake and blushed.

"Better to be here than out in the street," the woman pointed out.

"Juana said not to make the boy more timid than he is already." Becky's teeth ripped through a roll.

"I imagine the 'boy' has more worldly experience than his nursling appearance suggests." Marian leaned back. "Am I right, Mr. — what was your name?"

"Alderdice." Jake's shoulders stiffened as he put the coffee cup in Geneva's hands.

"How old are you?" Becky scrutinized him.

"Twenty-one."

"A splendid age." The woman tossed back a few dark curls falling into her face.

"For a young man," Marian said. "For a young woman — ah, that's different." She watched as Jake led Geneva to the settee. "You're nice-looking and obviously educated. Learn well, Geneva." She gave the girl a stinging glance. "Not all men are brutes." Becky's giggle clamored like a bell.

The young woman's eyes flashed at her elder. "I've known a few genteel men."

"In Flesa?" Becky scoffed. "That place is no better than a snake pit."

"That's not true!" Geneva set down the coffee cup at the edge of the table. Her skin was almost transparent, like the dragonflies he had seen in the woods with only their eyes showing life. The girl could not have been older than sixteen.

"My grandfather came from Flesa," he said kindly. "He became one of the most prominent businessmen in San Francisco."

"Exactly my point." Marian gave him a keen glance. "A man is luckier than a woman."

"One needs more than luck to get out of Flesa," Becky remarked.

"Leave her alone!" he snapped.

"Chivalry and manners," Becky observed with a smile. "My dear Geneva, you're getting on in the world."

"Don't be cruel, dear." Marian said. "The girl's been ill."

"She oughtn't to be here, then!" In a voice riddled with anguish, she said, "We'll take up a collection for you, Geneva.

Juana is sure to contribute. I know of a sanatorium up in Pasadena—"

Geneva gazed down at the cup in her hands. Becky slumped back in her chair, looking worn and brittle.

The doors opened, and Juana came in with Stevens. Both had smiles on their faces.

"Ladies, we shall finally have some decor on that wall over there." Turning to Jake, she added, "You have a fine talent, Mr. Alderdice. Mr. Stevens has just been showing me."

Jake thanked her, feeling bewildered.

"I believe we can find a hammer and some nails for you," the woman continued.

"Ma'am?"

"For the paintings." The woman laughed. "Harland, I think you had better explain. Your friend is liable to faint. Artists can be very dramatic sometimes."

"Jake is no longer an artist," said Stevens in a quiet voice.

"Then we shall value his work all the more," Juana said.

"You're most kind, ma'am," Jake murmured.

More ladies entered the parlor as he and Stevens hung the paintings on the wall. His apprehension disappeared as he saw in the women's eyes the admiration he had been seeking. They smiled as their fingers brushed the painted trees and the birds and clouds. Juana beamed like a proud mother.

Stevens whispered, "No doubt Culver would glare and complain about the indignity of it."

"He would prefer to see them in some swell's parlor," Jake agreed.

The redhead snorted. "If this isn't swell enough, I don't know what is!"

Geneva was one of the last to approach the display. Shadows fell across her face, making her skin sallow even under the brilliant light. Her eyes looked enormous inside her skeletal face. Suddenly, she let out a screech. He caught her by the shoulders, and she collapsed in his arms, sobbing. Marian and Becky helped her out of the room.

Juana was the first to break the silence that followed. "It was the girl in the painting. The tragedy of a child who remembers being a child."

On their way home, Jake realized the irony of her words. Geneva was still a child in many ways, but her innocence remained a memory stirred by his child Diana.

CHAPTER 24

When Jake went for a walk on the beach at dawn the next day, he was surprised to see the boardwalk crowded with people.It was as if in these last dying weeks of summer, the resort guests were determined to exploit every minute they could. He strolled past the hotels and reached the ghost ship. A mist surrounded the anvil-shaped bow, defying the assault of sea water that kept trying to break it down. He suddenly wished Geneva was with him. She would find strength in the monster's resilience. As Stevens had said, it would survive long after any of its observers. He gave it an absentminded salute.

"The lofty beast has earned your respect, I see." Stevens was beside him. He looked awkward in his dark suit, starched white shirt, and stiff tie. The short beard he had grown shone glossy against the calm sea.

"How did you know I was here?"

Stevens turned around "You forget Diana always finds her prey."

Vivian stood a little distance away stabbing into the sand with the edge of her parasol. The redhead called out in a grand voice,

"You suspected your brother was up to some mischief so you followed him?"

She glared. "I trust my brother, Mr. Stevens. But I saw you following him."

"And you don't trust me." The redhead eyed her. "Still."

Vivian made a circle in the sand.

Stevens watched her for a moment. "You may think better of me when you hear I decided to follow your advice."

She looked up. "What advice?"

"You suggested Maestro might not be happy among strangers, and I've concluded you were right. I'm taking him to Neart Castle."

"I'm glad to hear it."

Stevens turned to Jake. "I was hoping I could entice you to join me. I've something to show you I'm sure will interest you."

Vivian raised her parasol over her head. The sharpness of her blue eyes competed with the brilliant sea. "I'm eager to see this humble abode of yours too, Mr. Stevens."

For the first time since Jake had known him, the redhead was stunned. "The house is not at its best in the summer," he lamented. "The servants get rather lazy, and my mother has trouble attending to them properly."

"We're all more lax in the summer, aren't we?" Vivian smiled.

"Still, I don't think you would find it interesting."

"I do already," she insisted. "From what little you've told us, I find it fascinating."

"Don't be a nuisance, Viv." Jake felt Stevens' anxiety mounting. "It's inconvenient."

"It doesn't seem like an inconvenience for you to go." Her eyes flashed.

"You're brother's right, Miss Alderdice," said Stevens. "I meant this as an informal invitation for Jake. My mother is not receiving today, you see."

"I don't ask to see your mother," she said. "Not that I wouldn't be pleased to meet her and your father."

Jake's veins pulsated in his neck. "You're not invited, Viv."

She tilted the parasol. She looked like a porcelain doll with her face sweet and light and her eyes wide and appeasing. "Mr. Stevens, you wouldn't break a promise to me, would you?"

He stared. "I beg your pardon?"

"You promised you would arrange for me to meet your father," said Vivian. "So I could judge for myself if he is a tyrant."

"Don't be rude, Viv!" Jake snapped.

"You haven't forgotten, have you?" She stared at the redhead.

Stevens' stormy mood eased. "No, Miss Alderdice, I haven't forgotten. Let it never be said I don't keep my promises to a lady."

"If it's too much trouble, Stevens—"

"On the contrary," said the redhead. "Your sister's presence might add an interesting spark."

"Is home so dull for you, Mr. Stevens?" Vivian asked.

"Not dull, Miss Alderdice. A little unsettling at times."

She glanced down at the sand. "I can understand that."

They did not take the Brata. Stevens rented a barouche painted black with red wheels. He drove it himself, expertly maneuvering the horses along the pebbled road. Jake and Vivian sat in back with Maestro in his sister's lap. The pup seemed content to be leaving Waxwood as he submitted to Vivian's caresses with glee. Vivian wrapped the scarf closer around her head, her face shrinking inside the blue and gold silk.

They soon veered off into a narrower road. The redhead talked about the valley near his home, describing animals he had seen in the animated way of one who had made a study of them for years.

"You speak as if you created them yourself," Vivian remarked.

"Do you think me so presumptuous as to see myself as a God or conjurer?"

"The word that came to my mind was egotist," she said pleasantly.

Jake winced, but Stevens laughed. "Perhaps I am, a little. I've lived in my castle all my life, and this valley was my kingdom when I was a boy."

"You must have been very lonely," she said in a soft voice.

"I was solitary," the man admitted. "Always looking to escape."

"From whom?"

"I don't know, really," the man lamented, but Jake felt he was lying. "The same sort of person you and your brother we're escaping from, I imagine."

"How do you know Jake and I were escaping from anyone?" she challenged.

"I keep my eyes and ears open, Miss Alderdice," he answered.

"Walking into other people's private moments," Jake murmured.

Stevens either did not hear him or chose to ignore the comment. "Men like your grandfather can be difficult to live with."

"How do you know what my grandfather was like?" She asked.

"I can guess what sort of person he was," said the redhead.

"Now you are being presumptuous," she snapped.

The redhead slipped a cigarette from his pocket while one hand grasped the reins. "I'm sorry you feel that way. I had hoped to become a friend of the family."

Without looking away from Maestro, Vivian said, "Tell me about your family."

"I told you once," he said. "My father is a very accomplished man, successful in his line of work and well-respected in his community."

"You sound like an obituary," she remarked. "I want to know what he's *really* like."

"He's a tyrant, according to you," said Jake dryly.

"I never said that," his sister snapped. "What sort of man is he?"

"He enjoys the outdoors," said Stevens. "He's rather passionate about Neart Castle. When he first came to America, Hale County was hardly more than wilderness and cliffs. He helped make it livable."

"So he's not a slave to his business, like our grandfather?" Vivian asked.

"When he was a young man, of course," said the redhead. "Now, he divides his time between his civic duties, his hunting, and his books."

"He reads?" Vivian looked surprised.

"He's quite a scholar." Stevens smiled. "He's done several translations of Gaelic legends. He has quite a collection in his library."

"I shall look forward to seeing it," said Vivian honestly. "And your mother?"

The carriage slowed at a fork in the road. When they were trotting again the redhead replied in a cautious voice, "What about her?"

"What are her interests?"

The man's profile became stiff and grievous. "My mother is not well."

"I'm sorry to hear it," said Vivian. "Perhaps some feminine company will cheer her up."

"I doubt that would be possible," said the redhead. "She prefers to remain in her room."

"I won't disturb her," Vivian promised. "I only meant I shall be glad to offer her some company."

"She has company," he said roughly. "My father spends a lot of time with her."

Vivian gave a coarse laugh. "I meant womanly company, Mr. Stevens. Sometimes it's difficult to unburden one's soul to a man."

"What makes you think her soul is burdened?" He made the turn a little too sharply.

"I know women like her," she said, her voice soft.

The redhead seemed touched by this. "Mother sometimes comes down for tea. Perhaps you'll meet her then."

"I'd like to," said Vivian. "Very much."

Stevens took out another cigarette. Jake observed his hand shake as he held the pocket lighter up to the tip.

CHAPTER 25

The town of Hale greeted them with a scent of herbs and flowers. Stevens grew visibly tense as he slowed the horses for some people crossing the street. They nodded at the redhead. He did not return the greeting.

"Do you know those people, Mr. Stevens?" Vivian asked.

"I've lived here all my life," he answered.

"That doesn't answer my question." She watched as a trio of ladies fluttered down the street.

"I know them well enough." The redhead cracked the reins, and the horses hurried down the road.

"You don't really belong, do you?" Jake brushed the dampness from his forehead.

Stevens grimaced. "Not anymore."

"Then why do you live here?" Vivian asked. "I imagine most men prefer their own lodgings."

"I don't live here, Miss Alderdice," he said simply. "I live in the castle."

They turned into a private road lined with red dust and stones. The carriage rocked violently from the strong wind, and a line of sea formed below the cliffs. Oaks lined a coarse section of the path, and Jake grasped the seat. Soon the trees faded to reveal a castle sitting on the cliffs. The oaks Jake had thought magnificent now looked puny compared to the castle's fierce grandeur. Stevens drove the carriage through the gates embossed with NEART CASTLE in gold. A pack of hounds appeared out of nowhere, nipping at the horses' heels. Maestro began yipping, pressing close to Vivian's chest, looking up at her with his sodden eyes.

Stevens jumped out of the carriage to quiet the hounds. The dogs pressed their noses against Jake's legs as he helped his sister down, her hands clutching Maestro. The hounds growled at Vivian with suspicion and glared at the shivering pup.

"I apologize," said Stevens. "Dogs are a little wary of new additions."

"They don't like women much either," Vivian said dryly.

"They're not used to women, Miss Alderdice."

"They see your mother, don't they?" Vivian grasped the edge of her skirt.

"She would hardly have much to do with them." The redhead shouted at the animals, and they cowered in silence. Stevens called for Mr. McFarland and a heavy-set man appeared. The redhead spoke to him in a low voice. He held out his arms. "Mr. McFarland will find a place for Maestro."

"A safe place, I hope." She held the pup close to her chest.

The man laughed. "T'will be all his own, don't you worry none."

The floor of the castle felt cool against his heels as they walked down the hall. The air was hollow and dusty, and paltry sunlight streamed from the windows. A chill wind brushed against his face.

Stevens threw open a closet door and removed two capes. "It gets rather drafty here, even in summer. But the garden is quite pleasant."

They followed the redhead through echoing chambers of

stone and brick. Vivian let the scarf fall around her neck. Strands of hair escaped the twisted braid and spilled over her shoulders. She looked like a child who had been playing all day, the graveness of life forgotten.

Stevens' eyes were approving. "I hope my home impresses you favorably, Miss Alderdice."

"It impresses me," she admitted.

"But not favorably?"

"I wonder what ghosts are hiding beyond the walls of this ancient place," she murmured.

"You're interested in ghosts, aren't you?" Stevens asked with a note of amusement. "Your brother told me about your specter."

She glared at Jake but said nothing.

The hallway ended in a pair of heavy doors. Stevens knocked lightly, then a little harder. Jake heard nothing, but the redhead opened both doors and ushered them inside. It was a massive room with a high ceiling and a wall of books. The spines stood out with imprinted letters Jake couldn't make out.

"Gaelic," Stevens whispered.

A man was sitting at an elevated desk with his back to them. Stevens cleared his throat, and the man turned. Jake knew he was Stevens' father. Mr. Stevens' stature was narrower than his son's and his shoulders were squarer. His face was marked with grim lines. His features were paler and rougher than his son's.

Stevens' debonair charm disappeared, and he looked like a child who hoped he had done right, with his hands twisted behind his back. Vivian studied the redhead with a twisted smile as if she were enjoying his discomfort.

Mr. Stevens motioned toward a few leather chairs. Vivian sat upright, her hands in her lap, grasping the handle of the parasol as if prepared to use it as a weapon. Jake fit himself awkwardly into the seat beside her. Stevens remained standing.

Mr. Stevens continued looking over his papers for a few more minutes before he pushed them aside and sat back, regarding them with inquiring eyes. His expression changed to a tired patience, like someone who was often faced with inferiors. Jake doubted the man had ever received a kind word in his life, nor ever gave one.

"Father, this is Jake Alderdice," Stevens said. "I told you about him." Mr. Stevens bowed. "This is his sister, Vivian. She decided to join us at the last moment."

A look of annoyance crossed Mr. Stevens' face. "Delighted, I'm sure, Miss Alderdice."

"Your son didn't tell us we would be disturbing you." Vivian glared at the redhead.

"Not at all, not at all."

Jake mumbled. "We won't take up any more of your time."

Mr. Stevens studied him. "Harland tells me you're an artist."

"Not anymore, sir," Jake mumbled.

The man threw a glance at his son. "I thought you told me you were helping this young man in his work."

"His grandfather's business, sir," said Stevens. "Jake is the grandson of Malcolm Alderdice."

"Ah, yes, good man, good man." Mr. Stevens' quick eye accosted Jake. "So you've settled down and given up this nonsense about painting, eh?"

"It wasn't nonsense, Mr. Stevens," Vivian said. "It was my brother's dream since he was a boy."

Mr. Stevens did not look at her, but stormy aversion replaced his impassioned expression. "A young man your age has a duty to himself and his family and his community. Isn't that so, Harland?" He shot his son a look.

"Yes sir," said the redhead.

Vivian wandered over to the bookshelves.

"Jake still draws, Father," the redhead ventured. "He does very interesting work. He did a splendid drawing of Roger."

The man's thick eyebrows shot up. "You must show me some time, Mr. Alderdice."

The book Vivian was holding dropped to the floor. She bent down to retrieve it, but Stevens reached it first and slipped it back on the shelf. "I don't think you would like my brother's work, Mr. Stevens," she said in a steady tone. "Jake favors myth and fantasy."

"The fantastical has always intrigued me," said Mr. Stevens. "As long as it doesn't go too far astray." The hushed room grew more oppressive. The older man boomed, "Have you ever gone hunting, Jake?"

"No, sir."

"Our grandfather never had much time for such nonsense." Vivian said pointedly as she returned to her chair, her figure more upright than before.

"It's not nonsense to many men, Viv," Jake said in a low voice.

"Quite right, lad," said Mr. Stevens. "You're young, but ambitious, I've no doubt." He gave him a menacing smile.

"Jake is modest as well," Stevens added.

"Modest!" The man scoffed. "There's a time for modesty and a time for boasting, even in one so young. I hope you're teaching him to be discerning of both, Harland." He shot his son another look.

"Yes, sir," said the redhead.

The man rose. "Hunting can very well be your best teacher."

"I mean to take it up, sir," Jake said. "Stevens — Harland — promised to take me." He felt his sister's eyes on him.

He turned to his son. "Show Mr. Alderdice the trophy room. I'm sure he'll find it inspiring."

"Trophy room?" Vivian eyed the man. "It sounds rather morbid."

"Yes, well," Mr. Stevens grumbled, "I hardly think it would interest a woman."

"I am an uncommon woman, Mr. Stevens," said Vivian. "As your son will tell you."

The man gave her a look and turned to Jake again. "You must

join us during the hunting season." He looked at Stevens with a wink. "A straight shot on a bear will rid you of your bashfulness, young man."

"My brother's modesty isn't a flaw, Mr. Stevens," snapped Vivian.

The older man continued as if she hadn't spoken, "I'm sure you'll take to it just as Harland did."

"Very kind of you to invite me," Jake said.

"Well, well, glad to have met you." He pumped Jake's hand vigorously.

Vivian rose. "Do you know, Mr. Stevens, I made a prediction about what kind of man you were based on what your son told us about you?"

"Indeed?" The man's eyebrow arched.

"We ought to have bet money on it. I would have won." She sauntered out of the room.

As Mr. Stevens watched her leave, his pale face drained into a furious red flush, and his eyes fired with animosity. He began picking through the papers with deliberate fervor.

CHAPTER 26

As Stevens led them down the stairs, he threw Vivian a look. "You're too bold, Miss Alderdice."

"I speak my mind, Mr. Stevens," she said. "You ought to know that by now."

"You were disrespectful, Viv." Jake snarled. "Mother would have been ashamed of you."

"He wasn't very pleasant to me, was he?" Vivian snapped. "He treated me worse than he probably treats his dogs."

"He might have been kinder if you hadn't been so caustic," he retorted.

"I wouldn't have been caustic if he would have treated me like a human being!"

The redhead studied her. "So you think you were right in judging my father a tyrant?"

Jake saw his sister glance down at her hands. "I shouldn't have said he was a tyrant. But he frightens me."

"I saw nothing frightening about him," Jake insisted.

"I don't deny he can intimidate people." The redhead admitted. "But I don't think I've ever heard any woman speak to him quite like that."

"Then it's about time one did."

Stevens laughed. "Shall I call the maid to take you into the garden?"

"Why only me?"

"I'd like to show your brother a few of the other rooms."

"I'd like to see them too." Her eyes sparkled.

Jake glared at her. "You weren't invited in the first place."

She gave him a crooked smile. "I'd like to see what Mr. Stevens is so anxious to show you."

"I've no objection," said the redhead. "In fact, I'm interested to hear what you think of our collection."

"Collection?"

"I intend to show you the gun room." He grinned.

Steep stairs opened into a narrow and dusty room. Revolvers and rifles rested on their heels, their sides hollow like gaunt cheeks. Jake watched Stevens weave his way around the racks, pointing to certain firearms and explaining them. Vivian followed close behind.

They reached the back of the room. The redhead's eyes were glassy as the sunlight shredded through the window above. "These are our iron beauties." He pointed to a row of rifles.

The muscles of Vivian's face tightened. "You speak of guns like they're works of art."

"They are, Miss Alderdice," said Stevens. "Some are true masterpieces of craftsmanship."

Jake approached the rack. A rifle jutted out as if challenging him to take it up.

"I don't like them." Vivian shuddered.

"Don't you?" Stevens said.

She glared at him.

"Have you ever tried to shoot one, Miss Alderdice?" A\ smile played on his lips.

She turned and headed toward the door.

"I would be most happy to teach you," Stevens called after her.

Vivian glanced at a display case near the door. She choose a gun carved in pale gold with a pearl black handle.

"You have excellent taste." The redhead grinned. "A lethal pistol. A woman's gun." He darted forward. "My father bought it for my mother, but she didn't take to it. I think you might, though. I think you just might."

Jake found his voice. "I don't think Vivian finds that amusing, Stevens."

His sister's fingers curled around the handle as she stared down at it. She put the gun back in its box and closed the case with a snap. "I want to go back to the hotel."

Stevens' mocking eyes melted. "Let me call the maid to take you to the garden. I'm sure you shall enjoy the flowers and the fruit trees. I believe Mother mentioned the orange tree is in bloom." He lingered near the doorway until the maid arrived and escorted Vivian down the stairs.

"I believe you really frightened her," Jake remarked.

"We're the ones who should be frightened," said the redhead. "I've seen what a woman can do with a gun." His pale face was dull against the cold. He motioned for Jake to follow him. In the back of the room, he pulled open a cabinet, exposing a hidden panel where a rifle lay on the floor. "It's yours."

Jake picked it up. The Winchester they had seen at the gunsmith's rested easily against his arm.

"It's loaded, of course." His eyes were wet like black ink. "I told Lorimar to arrange for a hunt this weekend."

"I don't know if I'm ready." A shiver went down Jake's spine.

Stevens gripped his forearm. "You're not saying you don't want to go?"

"I shall make a fool of myself."

"Hunting isn't a competitive sport, like Roger's barbaric football," said the redhead. "It takes intelligence, skill, and patience."

Jake tried to smile. "I have all three."

"Good." Stevens patted him on the back. "I'll lend you my copy of Roosevelt's *The Wilderness Hunter*. It ought to get you started." He led Jake outside. "Now you must see the trophy room. My father insisted, after all."

Jake followed the redhead down a winding gravel path. Some hounds clamored around them. Jake looked at their flat muzzles and the lean strength in their legs and thought about Maestro.

They reached several small buildings that stood apart from the castle. They stepped inside one decorated with the mid-Victorian pomp his grandfather had worshiped. The parlor threw colors from stained-glass windows onto the Oriental rug, while a bronze statue of herons reigned over the fireplace. The birds looked as if they would dart over his head and break through the window at any moment. The setting was so perfectly Alderdice that Jake could almost see Grandfather leaning against the mantel with his walking stick in his hand and his lips curved with the assured grin of one who belonged there.

"The trophy room is in here," said Stevens, his hand on a doorknob. "Mother insisted we keep it out of the castle." Grimness replaced his earlier mirth.

As his eyes adjusted to the blackness of the room, Jake was face to face with a grizzly bear. Its brown coat bristled and its sharp claws pointed directly at him. Its teeth pierced out of the open jaw with more helplessness than rage.

"It's real," Stevens murmured.

A lion spread out on the floor like a rug. An antelope with a crown of antlers fit neatly into the corner. Smaller animals dominated the rest of the room. Each one had a plaque nailed on a stand engraved with bold letters. *Harland, age 12, Big Sur. Harland, age 10, Maine. Harland, age 9, Canada.*

Stevens was watching him, his lips thin, and his hands folded. "My father had them mounted and labeled."

"You don't sound proud of it," Jake observed.

"I'm not," said the man.

Jake breathed. "He must have been very proud of you."

"He was." The redhead strolled to the window, his hands laced behind his back. "I was a crack shot by the age of eight." The lines deepened on his face. "Are you inspired?"

"I don't know." Jake felt uneasy. "Their expressions are rather jarring."

"That startled look," the redhead agreed. "The taxidermist's interpretation under my father's direction." He turned around, his hands still behind his back. "Do you know why I'm showing you this room?"

"Because you thought I would be inspired, like your father," Jake said.

"Inspiration is exactly what I don't want you to get from it."

"I don't understand, Stevens." He held his hand to his forehead.

"You're disgusted by it, aren't you?" He gave him a fervent look. "I wanted you to be disgusted. With your artistic nature, I knew you would see through this morbid display."

The animals' suspended animation increased Jake's unease and he edged toward the door. "If you find all this sickening, why are we going on a hunt this weekend?"

"We don't kill for gratification and glory," the redhead declared. "We hunt with dignity and respect for the animals we kill."

Jake looked at him with incredulousness. "Is there such a thing?"

"Certainly there is." The man's voice rose. "Before I became a part of the order, I was as proud as my father. Now I feel as disgusted as you do."

Jake's eyes caught the bear's. They were equals now, as the bear's frozen state had more life than most of the men he knew on Washington Street. "I'll remember that, Stevens."

They returned to the castle. The redhead was enthusiastic as he described the garden that looked out to the sea. As they moved toward the French doors leading outside, a canary-like woman sailed out of a room. The redhead caught her, and she struggled under his grip as if determined to use every bit of strength to get away.

"Mother!" Dazed, she peered up at him. "I thought you were having tea in the garden with Miss Alderdice."

"Tea?" She blinked. "Is it that time?" She waved at nothing. "I was just going, dear. I couldn't remember — yes, that's just where I was going." She looked up at her son as if he had just given her a reason to live.

Stevens' smile showed warmth and patience. "This is my friend, Jake Alderdice."

Mrs. Stevens turned her blinking eyes on Jake. "He looks like a nice boy."

"He's hardly a boy, Mother." Her son chuckled.

This seemed to distress her so much that Jake took her arm with the delicacy he reserved for wounded animals. "I'm only twenty-one, Mrs. Stevens."

She stared at him. In a loud voice, she called, "Fine weather we're having, isn't it?"

"You have a pleasant breeze here," Jake answered.

"You ought to wear your shawl, Mother," said her son.

She looked confused for a moment, then giggled. This sudden burst of girlishness smoothed away the wrinkles on her face. She looked twenty years younger. "You naughty boy, you're teasing me." She patted his cheek.

Jake watched the redhead's features fall, nearly ripping his reserve apart.

"May I get your shawl for you?" He moved toward the open doorway, but Stevens grabbed his arm.

"I'll get it."

The woman's hand clasped Jake's. "He's been showing you that nasty little room, hasn't he? I put my foot down, you know. Have it if you must, I said, but this is my house, *my* house, and I'll be damned if—" She giggled again. "I shouldn't say such words in front of the child. But he's not a child any longer. Is he?" Her eyes rose to the ceiling, and Jake realized the child was in her mind's eye.

"It's all right, dear." Stevens placed the shawl lovingly over his mother's thin shoulders.

"I stood my ground," she insisted.

"Margaret!" Mr. Stevens' broad figure stood in the dim hallway. "How many times have I told you not to bother people with your prattle?"

"Prattle. Yes." Mrs. Stevens let go of Jake's hand. "Always prattle." In a shrill voice, she added, "But only to dead walls, dead walls!" She darted back into the room and slammed the door.

Mr. Stevens' imposing figure vanished, and the hallway was undisturbed as if he had never been there at all.

"Poor Mother," the redhead sighed. "She's been in some state of confusion ever since I can remember."

Jake imagined the woman fluttering around in her vacant room like a hummingbird.

That evening, Larissa pried them with questions about Neart Castle.

"It's a place like any other, Mother." Jake played with the cake on his plate.

"I wish you were more observant," His mother sighed.

"I thought my problem is that I'm too observant."

"Not in about the right things." Larissa reached for the pitcher of cream.

"I shall pay more attention in future," Jake promised.

His sister had been unusually silent all evening, but now, she said, "Do you know what he is, Mother?"

"Your brother?" Their mother gave her a funny look.

"No," said Vivian. "*Him*."

"If you mean Stevens, say so," Jake snapped.

"You think he's such an admirable man," Vivian continued.

"Admirable and lonesome," said Larissa in a pointed tone.

"He's an animal!" She spat the words out.

"He'll hear you." Jake glanced at Stevens still lingering at his table, his congenial features gathered in deep thought.

"I don't care if he does," his sister declared. "He showed us a room full of rifles and revolvers, Mother. He wanted to show me how to shoot a pistol!"

Larissa flushed with displeasure, but quickly said, "I'm sure he was teasing you, dear."

"He was *not* teasing!" Vivian threw down her napkin. "I thought there were no more savages left in the world."

"I should think your suffragist friends would approve," his mother said dryly. "They might see it as part of the emancipation of womanhood."

"Perhaps you'd like me to bring you a few heads of deer under Mr. Stevens' excellent tutelage?" Vivian said in a crisp voice. "Or would you prefer the head of his insipid cousin?"

"Don't be gruesome, Vivian," Larissa snapped.

"There's nothing wrong with hunting," Jake insisted, thinking of the Order. "It builds a man's character and strength."

"So does heaving a piano out the window, but I shouldn't advise it," Vivian remarked.

"You don't understand, Viv," he said.

"Perhaps I do." She gave him a meaningful look. "Too well."

He sat in the lobby after dinner trying to read the Roosevelt book Stevens had given him, but he kept hearing her words: *I thought there were no more savages* There *had* been something savage in the eyes of those trophy animals. Now he read of Teddy Roosevelt praising the virtues of what his sister called savagery. The words fell from the page:

In hunting, the finding and killing of the game is after all but a part of the whole. The free, self-reliant, adventurous life, with its rugged and stalwart democracy; the wild surroundings, the grand beauty of the scenery, the chance to study the ways and habits of the woodland creatures — all these unite to give to the career of the wilderness hunter its peculiar charm.

His knees gave a little start as he thought of the men of the Order of Actaeon.

The book dropped from his lap. He bent down to retrieve it and read:

The chase is among the best of all national pastimes; it cultivates that vigorous manliness for the lack of which in a nation, as in an individual, the possession of no other qualities can possibly atone.

He shut the book. The words read like a nightmarish prophecy.

He wandered to the library, expecting to see the same elderly man who occupied it in the evenings and always looked at him as if he had interrupted a pleasant reverie. The room was empty except for a man bent over a stack of pages on the desk. When the man's head shot up, he saw it was Stevens. The redhead's features were gathered with the concentration that had plagued him at dinner.

"You're just in time." His impish grin was different from his usual good humor. "I need another pair of eyes for my project."

"Project?"

"Charter, then." Stevens handed him a page. "I'm eager to hear your thoughts."

Jake read:

<u>The Order of Actaeon Principles and Philosophies</u>

THE ORDER OF ACTAEON was established in 1871 in opposition to the disturbing inclination of modern young men toward falling into the trap of profit-seeking and vicious competition characteristic of civilized life and thus losing their manly strength and virtue. Modern man is going against the true nature of man to dominate and be in harmony with Nature.

To this end, the activities of this order shall evolve around three principles:

- Athletic prowess that builds strength and endurance
- Dominance of nature that fosters success and control

- Peaceful fraternity that encourages brotherhood
  and aid

All activities of the Order shall be guided by the following principles:

- That the Order shall comprise of older men (called "Patriarchs") who display the courage, cunning, and virility necessary to guide younger men (called "Youths") on their road to manhood. Any young man who takes the oath of the Order shall have but one guide.
- That any Youth brought into the Order shall have a sponsor to vouch for his trustworthiness and solidity.
- That a Patriarch may punish his Youth if he transgresses the rules or endangers the well-being of himself or his fellow brothers in any way he sees fit so long as the punishment is just and valid.
- That the secrecy of the Order and its activities shall be maintained at all times.
- That the activities of each man in his civilized life shall remain pertinent only to himself.
- That each man shall choose a name by which he will be known only to the Order.
- That we shall use what Nature offers but with respect and dignity toward Her power.
- That there shall be no spirit of competition among us. There shall be instead the spirit of fraternity and brotherhood, and any man may come to the aid of another.

- That each man shall pledge a life of purity as much as he is able among incorruptible Nature when he is with the Order.
- That each man shall take part in hunting parties organized by the Order, and that each Youth shall let his Patriarch guide him in the development of his strength, aggression, pride, and self-control.
- That each man shall hunt only for food and not for glory, and shall engage in ethical hunting as much as possible.

Each man shall adhere to the following philosophies and hold them to be just and good:

- That modern masculinity has become corrupt and is in need of purity to insure future success for himself and his brothers.
- That the manly virtues of restraint, grace, and morality upheld by our forefathers must be maintained and enhanced with power, aggression, and force.
- That emotional attachments drain a man of his intelligence and virility, and therefore, he is to maintain some distance between himself and others.
- That modern man is forced to separate his pure life from his civilized life for the sake of his virtue and well-being.

Any man who fails to recognize these principles and philosophies may be voted out of the Order by the council.

· · ·

"Wordy, perhaps." The redhead leaned his chair back. "But clear."

Jake dropped the parchment on the desk. "Doesn't the Order already have a charter?"

"They have nothing, friend," said Stevens. "That's why I took it upon myself."

Jake hesitated. "Won't it compromise the secrecy of the Order to have its principles and philosophies in writing?"

"You heard Lorimar say we maintain our past so we can know our future." Stevens' voice hardened. "What better way than with a secret charter buried underground with the guns?"

Jake reached into his pocket for a handkerchief. The room felt dark and close. Stevens watched him as he wiped his forehead. The man snapped window open.

"It was getting rather hot in here," Stevens said in a steady voice.

"I wasn't hot," Jake insisted.

"What do you think of my charter?"

"I think you ought to ask Lorimar and Smith—"

"It's done." The redhead's voice cut through the still air. "I shall present it to them tomorrow."

Jake laced his hands together. "I should think it was the council who must draw up a charter if they chose."

"I shall be one of the council soon." Stevens strolled to the bookcase, glancing at the spines. "I see you've been reading Teddy Roosevelt. Enlightening, isn't he?"

"He's quite an orator," Jake admitted.

"Eloquent and self-assured as any powerful man," the redhead agreed. "There are rumors he will run for governor now that the war in Cuba is over. With God's will, he may even run for president."

"I thought you didn't believe in God," Jake remarked.

Stevens whirled around. "My objection is to religion, not God." He fingered the spine of a book. "Pure man's world is at one with a higher being, though not in supplication. I ought to have added that to the charter."

"You're very devoted to the Order, aren't you?"

An insect entered the open window and buzzed about. The lights gave a bright glaze to the worn furnishings, and the flit of the insect's wings were visible as elongated shadows on the wall.

Stevens' hushed voice floated across the room. "I discovered them at the right time."

"What was the time?" Jake leaned forward.

"That's not a simple question to answer, friend," said the man.

"I'm still asking it."

Stevens returned to the desk. "I was eighteen and working down in the factory, as I told you. I used to go to the pubs with the Irish sailors sometimes after work."

"I can't imagine your father approved of that," Jake murmured.

The redhead glared. "I didn't always do what my father approved of back then." He continued in a dreamier tone, "A man walked in one nigh. He was in evening clothes and spoke with impeccable manners, which caused rather a stir. The men told me he was a swell who owned a string of fishing boats off the coast of Monterey."

"That doesn't seem like a swell's work to me," said Jake.

Stevens gave a deep chuckle. "The boats were mere play for him. He went out often with the fishermen."

"They told you this?"

"He told me."

"He was your friend."

"He ought to have been my rival," said the redhead. "He once did business with my father, but Father did him a nasty turn, and they became enemies."

"What was this man like?" Jake asked.

"A magnificent figure, dark and impeding. He could be tender too, though." The man looked at him with a grin. "He used to buy puppies by the litter and give them away to children."

"An interesting man," Jake remarked.

"The men said, 'Stay away from 'im, mate. Your pop ain't likely to 'predicate you messin' about with that bloke.'"

"But you did anyway?" Jake smiled a little.

Stevens raised his eyebrow. "I told you, I didn't always do everything my father's approved of." He cradled the back of his head in his hands. "The man told me stories about his exploits in the Civil War alongside Sherman and Grant. Not that he cared much for Grant in the White House." The redhead's eyes glazed over. "He loved hunting as much as I did."

"It was he who introduced you to the Order," Jake guessed.

"I was a young man aching for guidance, just as you are."

"Who was your Patriarch?" Jake asked.

Stevens looked at him with a smile. "The man I met, of course."

"And he was?"

"Allcock."

Jake glanced at the heart-shaped shadow of the fly's wings against the wall.

"He was a good man," said Stevens. "A big man like me, but he had the laugh of a child. He took me on safari with him in Africa."

"Yet he betrayed the Order."

The redhead was quiet for a moment. "He loved his wife. She was frantic about his disappearances when the Order arranged for activities that stretched over several days. She wouldn't believe his excuses. She was sick with worry over him. He had to tell her."

Jake heard a strange noise coming from the direction of the insect and he waved it out the window.

"Allcock understood," Stevens said. "He understood, and he left willingly. I think he was just tired." The man's eyes were dim. "He lost the will that had driven him to create the group in the first place. He lost it just as I was picking it up."

"Your purpose in life," Jake murmured.

"If you wish to call it that," said the redhead. He rose. "I must pack my things for tomorrow. We shall leave at eight. You continue to read your book, but not for too long. Mustn't be too tired in the morning." He grinned and strode out the door.

Jake sat for a while with the book in his lap. He dozed off and dreamed of Joseph Stevens glowering with rage while a defiant young Stevens stood opposite him, tall and crushing like Actaeon.

CHAPTER 28

The next morning, Jake came out into the hallway in his socks and carrying his shoes, intending on an early morning walk before meeting Stevens. He was startled to see Larissa elegantly dressed in pale violet. her blond hair covered with a modest hat.

"Good morning, Mother," he said a little tentatively.

"Where are you off to this time of the morning, Jacob?"

He tried to sound disinterested. "Stevens invited me to Neart Castle for the weekend."

"I hope you plan on dressing properly." She glanced down at the shoes in his hands.

"I won't disgrace you, if that's what you're worried about." He looked away.

"I hope not," she said. "Do be back by Sunday afternoon. We'll be catching the twelve-fifteen train on Monday back to the city, don't forget." She walked past him, the door closing softly behind her.

His hands shook with anger. Even though he was a man, his mother's belittlement still cleaved him to the bone.

His sister appeared draped in cambric with her slippers in hand.

"Sorry I woke you, Viv." He slid his foot inside the leather shoe.

She dropped on the couch beside him.

"I have things to do. Go away."

He put on the other shoe and leapt to his feet, knowing she would follow him. Reaching the stairs, he broke into a run. By the time his pounding feet reached the thick Waxwoodian carpet, he was a child again. There was no Larissa, no Washington Street, and no demands of any kind waiting for him. He was transported into a place only lonely children could understand.

He sailed past the hotel staff laying out the morning paper and darted out into the courtyard. The air brushed his face with refreshing dew. He reached the beach and whirled around, catching Vivian's arm. They were both out of breath and choking with laughter.

"You win." He collapsed on the sand, feeling ground shells scratch his head.

"Then give me a prize," his sister begged. "A walk on the beach. We haven't done that since we got here."

He could almost hear Smith snarling, *Woman is impurity defined*. He gazed up at her pleading eyes.

Vivian held his arm, her grip rigid, piercing through his skin. "You're wearing Grandmother's ring."

"I found it this morning," she said. "Grandfather gave her this ring in Waxwood." She sighed. "She was happy here."

"I don't know that, and neither do you."

"I do know, Jake," she said. "I know everything."

His chest tightened. "You mean because you went with Ruth that day seven years ago?"

The wind swept the hanging lace on her sleeves. "I've wanted to tell you for a long time. But I wasn't sure if you could endure it."

Jake's anger rose. "You and Mother keep treating me like a child."

"You're right, of course" she said. "And we shouldn't. You're a man now, and you've a right to know the truth." She sat down on one of the rocks.

He remained standing, his hands buried in his pockets. "Truth about what?"

"About what happened forty years ago."

"What does it matter now what happened forty years ago?"

"It affects us in the most insidious ways," she insisted. "And it will continue to do so if we turn a blind eye to it."

Two children shuffled close to them, then giggled and ran off.

Jake felt the wind cut into his shoulders. "This has to do with what Bertha Ross said at Grandmother's funeral, doesn't it?"

Vivian began the ladder with her hands. He realized for the first time how troubled she was.

"I was at that picnic too, Vivian," he said. "She was just a confused little woman living on her memories."

"She wasn't confused," said his sister. "She knew everything about Grandmother we didn't and should have."

"Don't talk in circles," he snapped.

"You know Grandmother took the name Grace when she was in Waxwood?" He nodded. "She didn't choose it. The young man with whom she fell in love gave it to her."

He shrugged. "That's hardly a revelation. Young women always have flirtations before they marry. You've had several yourself."

"His name was Evan."

A knot formed in his stomach. He remembered Mrs. Ross' cry: *I didn't say a word about Evan!*

"He was an artist who lived in Brandywine," Vivian continued.

"Who says she was in love with him?" Jake ran his hand over the rock. "They may have just been friends."

"There are letters," said his sister. "She was here over a year."

"So that was how Mrs. Ross knew all those strange stories about Grandmother," he murmured.

Vivian stopped the finger ladder and bent forward, raking the sand with her hand. "She stayed with the Rosses for a while before she went to be with Evan at Brandywine."

He looked sharply at her. "That's not what Mrs. Ross said."

"It's what the letters said," Vivian said. "She lived there with Evan, his sister, and his niece."

"Grandmother would never do that."

"He helped her see herself as an artist and not as an ornament," Vivian continued. "Is it any wonder she fell in love with him?"

"What does it matter now?" Jake insisted. "She married Grandfather, didn't she?"

"It was because of Evan that she married him."

He picked up a broken shell. "That makes no sense."

"Grandfather came along and destroyed their love." Her voice grated like the sand under his feet.

"Why shouldn't he?" Jake asked. "He told me once he loved Grandmother ever since he came to work for Carlyle Shipping. Why shouldn't a rising young man take an interest in his employer's daughter?"

"He came to convince her that Evan was a fiend, and she ought not to have anything to do with him," said Vivian.

"You're assuming too much," he said.

"I told you, Jake, it's in the letters!"

"And I suppose you're going to tell me now there's some deep, dark secret that is going to shake the Alderdice tree to its very roots." His voice cracked in the wind. "Really, Viv, you ought to be on the stage."

His sister took a handful of sand. A flat shell, oval and perfect remained in her palm. "Grandmother had a baby."

He laughed. "Of course she had a baby! What else would Mother have been forty years ago?"

"I meant she had a baby before she married Grandfather." Vivian's tone was severe. "Evan's baby."

A string of seaweed swept toward his feet, and he kicked it aside. "You're lying! Grandmother wasn't that sort of woman."

Now it was Vivian who laughed. "She was a woman just like any other, Jake. She wasn't the angel in the house."

"If what you say is true," he asked, "then what happened to this baby?"

"It died." Her voice softened.

"Was that in the letters too?"

"Mother told me."

"Mother!"

"She knows everything," said Vivian. "Evan wanted to marry her. He was willing to leave Brandywine and find work in the city."

"Grandmother would never have married such a man."

"She loved him, Jake," she said. "They would have married if it hadn't been for Grandfather."

He rose. "I don't want to hear any more."

"Can't you see, I'm trying to tell you how it really was!"

He stared hard at her. "You don't know how it really was."

"People said Grandfather was ruthless, but it was more than that." His sister's voice droned over the tossing waves. "As far as he was concerned, people were there to do with as he pleased. His will was theirs."

"He had courage," Jake insisted. "Grandmother chose him because she knew that."

"She chose him because she realized she was duty-bound to marry *somebody*."

"If Grandfather married her despite what she'd done, *he* was the one who really loved her, not Evan," said Jake.

"You don't know, Jake."

"Do you?" He eyed her.

"I know what Evan's niece Verina told me of him," said Vivian. "You ought to read the letters, Jake."

His arms felt heavy. "I've no wish to read letters written by dead people!"

"I put them in the playroom," Vivian said. "You know where."

He knew. The book bound with heavy leather and gold braids filled with strange mementos from the past. The Alderdice Family Dreambook. Once, he wished to know the riddles behind those family heirlooms. He had no desire to know now. "Let the letters stay locked with all the other dead memories."

"You can't take memories back because you don't like them," she snapped. "The truth is the truth, Jake."

"This is not truth," he cried. "This is digging up skeletons."

"That's what Verina said." Vivian sighed. "But the specters will hound your footsteps if you don't face them."

Savagery welled up inside him. "Grandfather was valiant, and I hope to God I'll be like him one day!"

Her hand reached his face. The slap stung like a hot iron. Her lips trembled in the sun. "Jake, I'm sorry!"

"I must go." He was no longer angry. Only dejected.

Her voice rose loud and desperate. "We haven't looked for sand dollars yet. Remember you promised you would find me a sand dollar, and we would bring it to Mother on a silver tray like a calling card? You said it would make her smile."

Without turning around, he said, "We were only children then, Viv."

He left her crouching down, her hands raking through the wet sand.

CHAPTER 29

"**Y**our silence is too exacting for my taste, friend," said the redhead as they rumbled down the road in the Brata. He reminded Jake of a woodsman with his beard bordering his angled face, and the sleepless suspicion glaring from his eyes.

Jake replied. "I've had some revelations."

"What sort of revelations?"

"That's none of your business!" Jake knew he had offended the man. "I'm sorry. Some things my sister said upset me."

"I thought it might have something to do with her." They passed a pair of kissing redwoods. "I saw you on the beach this morning."

"Vivian told me things—"

"Family secrets, you mean?"

Jake nodded. "About my grandparents."

"That can hardly touch you now."

Jake pressed his hand against the window. The wind kicked back against it. "'That emotional attachments drain a man of his intelligence and virility, and therefore, he is to maintain some distance between himself and others.'"

"I wasn't referring to that," said Stevens. "My father and his brother left everyone behind in Scotland. They never inquired about the family back home. My father said it wouldn't do to look back."

"You can't look back," Jake echoed.

The redhead eased the car into the clearing. The silence was deadening. "You're not looking back now, aren't you?"

"On the contrary." Jake looked into a veil of leaves. "I intend only to move forward."

Two retrievers ran to meet them as they approached the camp. The men were on the path, waiting for them. Stevens held up Jake's Winchester and waved it like a flag. "The Youth is with us," he shouted.

"A fine rifle, my boy, a fine rifle!" Smith's lips curved into a gnarling smile.

"Shall we take it out for a test?" The redhead asked.

Pines looked to Jake, "You don't want to go, do you?"

"Why wouldn't I?" Jake stiffened.

"You know the rules, Pines," Smith warned. "Every Youth attends the hunts." He turned to Stevens. "We spotted ducks near here earlier this morning."

As they headed into the wax woods, Jake saw Stevens hand the rolled up parchment to Lorimar and Smith. A feeling of dread assaulted the pit of his stomach.

The leaves were still gleaming with morning dew, and the redwoods watched over them like the eye of careful fathers. Jake felt the peacefulness of the forest. "Actaeon must have felt like this," he murmured.

"He's only a myth," Pines murmured.

"He was a hunter and a hero," Stevens declared. "We expect every Youth must respect him."

Pines clutched his rifle, his face white.

Stevens held Jake back as the other two advanced. "Aim high," he said in a quiet voice. "Look for the duck's head, and not its body. Shoot the moment you see it. That's the skill of hunting. You don't wait, but shoot."

"Don't wait, but shoot," Jake repeated.

The redhead leaned closer. "Never shoot a duck in a flock. That might hurt the other ducks." He let go of Jake's elbow and went on ahead.

Jake felt another hand grab his arm. He turned to stare into Pines' flame-blue eyes. "I was hoping I would never see you here again."

Jake's face grew hot. "Why wouldn't I come back?"

"You don't seem the type," said the young man.

"Neither do you," Jake pointed out.

The boy looked down at the ground.

They reached a heart-shaped pond with water lilies floating on the surface. A flash of red sailed through the air some distance away. Everyone was deathly silent. Lorimar motioned to Stevens, and the redhead steadied his rifle against his shoulder, pressed his cheek on the stock and fired. The duck dropped like a stone in the bushes a few feet away.

"We used to keep ducks on the farm." Pines' eyes grew misty.

One of the dogs emerged with the duck in his mouth. Stevens grabbed it and waved it at them with a wild grin.

"Good shot." Smith glanced at Jake. "You've an excellent teacher there, Carlyle."

"Sickening," Pines growled beside him.

Stevens dropped the bird and grabbed the boy's shoulders. His towering figure rose with the strength of his dark eyes. "What did you say?"

"He meant sickened, as in puny," Jake said in a quiet voice, "Not much meat."

Lorimar was behind him. "It will still make a good roast." He placed his hand on the redhead's shoulder. "Let him go, Duff."

Stevens released his grip and patted the young man on the back as he would have one of his hounds. "My apologies, Pines."

Jake could see the young man was trying to be cheerful, but his smile rang as false as the ease in his voice, "No harm done."

As they waited near the pond, Pines stuck close by him. The young man spoke in a hoarse whisper. "I brought some of my paintings to show you." Jake glanced at him. "They don't know," the boy continued. "I hid them in back of a hut."

"I thought we must keep our civilized lives hidden from members of the Order," Jake murmured.

The young man's eyes grew wistful. "We lived near Pine Lake in Colorado."

"Pines, I don't think you should—" Jake glanced at Stevens, who gave him an odd look but seemed more intent on watching the sky. "I thought you said you lived on a farm."

"That was afterward," said the young man. "We only lived in Colorado for a short time. He and Ma wanted to live with nature. It was so peaceful there."

"Memory paints a pretty picture," Jake lamented.

"I'm aware of that!" Pines' shriek broke the silence and earned him a vicious glare from his Patriarch.

Another bird came rambling through the sky. Smith gave Pines a quick nod, and the boy aimed at it, but missed.

"The head, the head!" Smith snarled. "How many times have I told you, aim for the head!"

Pines looked startled, but Jake guessed he was relieved he had missed the bird.

"Next time," Lorimar said in a soothing voice.

When the men resumed watch, Pines said in a hoarse whisper. "Sometimes, I wish I were a child again."

"What good would it do to be a child now?"

The young man grabbed his arm. "What are you doing here? What in hell are you doing here, Carlyle?"

Jake's hands tightened on the Winchester. "The same as you."

"No," said Pines. "Not the same. All my folks are dead. I got no one. You got people, I'll bet."

"A sister," Jake admitted. "A mother."

The young man's forehead creased with age. "Most of them don't have anyone worth going back to."

Smiths' words echoed in the soundless woods: *You must let go of everything that grows away from you.*

"They'll make you, you know." The young man's voice pricked his ears. "They'll make you give up everyone but them!"

"No one can do that," Jake whispered.

A buzzing noise came from the sky, and Stevens flicked his head at Jake.

The young man clawed Jake's arm. "Go back, I tell you. Go back!"

Jake raised his rifle and, when the bird neared his range, he aimed, trying to remember all Stevens had told him. As the shot rang he heard his grandfather's voice: *Go back, go back.*

The retriever brought back the bird, and Stevens grabbed it. "It's a coot!"

"I thought it was too small," Smith grumbled.

Jake stared at the bird lying in the grass, its red eyes wide and wings folded.

"It's his first bird, gentlemen," Lorimar pointed out. "Even a coot is something."

"I'm sorry." Jake felt his hands slip from the rifle.

"Don't worry, son," said the man. "We've all mistaken a coot for a duck at one time or another. Hard to tell at that distance."

The redhead's eyes burned with dark anger, like the eyes of an executioner. His voice rose, thick but soft, in the ashen light. "It was my fault."

"No one is to blame, Duff," said Lorimar. The men took their cue from him and offered silent sympathy.

As the men faded away, Stevens approached him. "It was a good first try, Jake. I know you've had your mind on other things."

"Yes," he said absently. "I've had my mind on other things."

"We ought to bury it," said Pines.

"Bury it? Hell, no, boy, we're going roast it!" Smith said with a laugh. "Just like Lorimar said, a coot is something, if you know how to cook it right."

Jake dropped to his knees beside the bird. Tears fell onto the crumpled feathers.

"Don't tell me you're grieving over a coot!" Cadden snorted.

"No, sir," said Jake. But he felt he had done a terrible wrong.

That night, the scents or roast duck and coot filled the village. The men built a bonfire, and its flames turned the night from beetle blue to sunset pink. Smith had brought a jug of homemade rye and passed it among them. Jake could not bring himself to drink after it had passed so many lips. Each time the jug was thrust at him, he gave it to the next man without looking at it. Stevens' disapproval pierced through the smoke.

After the meal, the men subdued from the liquor, Lorimar. The man rose and cleared his throat. "Gentlemen." His ragged voice wavered. "Gentlemen, Duff has been kind enough to set our doctrines down on paper, so we need never doubt what we stand for." He unrolled the parchment, handing it to his Youth, Drysdell. The young man's fish eyes devoured the writing on the page with the hunger of an emaciated dog. "Duff has asked to take his place in the council and has asked us to put it to a vote."

The forest was silent except for a scratching stick. Pines was making a cross in the dirt.

"I think you'll agree with me, gentlemen, that it's time," he continued. "Duff is one of our oldest members and has guided many of you here. His record of bringing in new recruits is unmatched."

"Hear, hear!" a few of the older men called, clapping their hands. A bird flew over the fire, looking for scraps, then thought better of it and headed toward the woods.

"His loyalty to the Order is resolute and sincere," Smith agreed.

"I think we all recognize Duff's dedication and leadership is what our order demands of a council member," Lorimar said.

Stevens' countenance showed the perfect balance of modesty and confidence. "I am truly honored, gentlemen."

The shrieking bird returned. "Loons came early this year," Pines remarked.

"Who the devil cares?" Rage made Stevens' face hollow against the fire.

The young man bent his head so low it was almost in his lap.

"Shall we put it to a vote?" Lorimar asked. There was a general murmur of ascent. "All in favor?" Every hand shot up except Pines'.

"Congratulations, Duff!" The man said, pumping his arm.

"Well-deserved, sir, well-deserved." Smith did likewise. Every man except Pines reached congratulated the redhead.

For the first time since Jake had known Stevens, he observed a shadow of anxiety cross his face. The redhead's countenance melted into the flames.

When the last of the fire had burned out, he and Stevens retreated to the house with the Swiss roof.

"You can stay with me, if you prefer," said Pines.

"He doesn't prefer," snapped the redhead.

The young man lingered for a few moments, then repeated to his own hut.

Stevens grabbed his arm, his fingers twisting into Jake's skin. "We're both moving forward, aren't we?"

"You're moving forward, not I." Jake did not look at him.

"What affects me, affects you, friend. When I rise, so do you."

"I thought the Actaeons believe in peaceful fraternity without competition," he said.

"It can't hurt to impress them, can it?"

"I'm not looking to impress anybody, Stevens," said Jake. "Is that your purpose now? To win the power of the Order?"

Stevens blew out the candle. "One pursues the most worthy prey when one goes after power."

Jake's mind echoed with words: *The chase is among the best of all national pastimes*. "And if we're chasing the wrong thing, Stevens?" he asked.

Stevens yawned. "When you become a man of business, you'll see I'm right."

Jake stared into the dark, the walls of the small, cold house closing in on him.

CHAPTER 30

When Jake finally dozed off, his fitful slumber turned into an ominous dream. He saw himself with a crossbow shooting at the moon. An owl fell to the ground. The bird shimmered in the moonlight, immobile and tearless. Then it spoke in a language not quite human, mumbling like a monk passing into grace. The owl spread its wings and, rose, its shimmering body flame-red, eyes large and diabolical. The screech escaping its mouth awakened Jake.

He sat up and looked out the window at the wax wood trees. It was still too dark to see more than their outline. He tried to speak but went into a coughing fit instead.

"Quiet!" A candle highlighted Stevens' imposing figure. The regal poise and self-assurance Jake admired had turned into apish savagery. His brutal gaze tore through Jake.

He brushed his eyes with his sleeve. "I was dreaming—"

Stevens set down his rifle, his face resembling his father's. "Get up. We're bringing breakfast back to camp."

Jake rose, his legs unsteady as a colt's. Pines' words echoed in the surrounding twilight: *Go back, I tell you, go back!*

Stevens snarled. "Remember what I said last night."

"I don't understand.

"You made am embarrassing mistake yesterday with the coot," said the redhead. "We must correct that mistake. Show them you're a hunter."

"A crack shot at the age of twenty-one?" Jake said warily, thinking of the day in the trophy room.

"Why not?"

The dream with the shimmering owl needled his mind. "And if I shoot the wrong prey?"

"You won't," said the redhead.

Jake remained in bed. Pines' warning made him shiver. "Stevens, is it true the Order encourages men to forsake all personal ties?"

The redhead settled his rifle over his shoulder. "You read the charter."

"So they advocate relinquishing all ties?"

The redhead grimaced. "Not all of them. You visited my house."

"Then what Pines told me isn't true." Jake breathed easier.

The man raised his eyebrow. "I must tell Smith about that boy."

Jake grabbed his wrist. "If he's asked to leave the Order, Smith will abandon him. He has no family, nowhere to go."

The redhead leaned against the wall. "We can't have a boy who mistrusts us, friend."

"I don't know if I could do it, Stevens."

"Do what?"

"Give up all ties."

The pale light caught Stevens' graceful face. "No tree ever grows on ground decayed by the past. You ought to know that better than anyone."

Through the gleaming candlelight that bounced against the glass, Jake caught another glimpse of the wax wood trees. His grandmother and grandfather appeared embedded in the bark, not as they were before they died but as they appeared in the daguerreotype taken soon after their honeymoon. His grand-mother was only twenty, her gaze frightened. His grandfather had been eight years older, his blue eyes piercing as stilettos. Stevens was right. The Alderdice family tree stood on decaying ground. He could make ti come alive again if he fulfilled the prophecy of his manhood.

He rose and reached for the Winchester lying on the ground. "Perhaps we can find a rabbit this time."

Stevens grinned. "I'll be waiting for you outside."

They went deep into the woods. Dark vegetation made the air heavy, and leaves and twigs brushed their shoulders. The redhead seemed intent on reaching a specific place, his gait fast and steady. Rodents and other small animals scampered around the shrubs and rosemary, peering at them as they passed.

They came to a stream lined with glittering rocks surrounded by a barrier of trees. The scent of wildflowers filled the air. Stevens held out his arm. A short distance away, a crack sounded from behind the shrubbery. "Might be a deer," he whispered.

Jake felt the dampness at the base of his neck. "That's big game. Perhaps we ought to go back for the others."

Stevens grabbed his arm, twisting it behind his back. Jake reeled at the redhead's ferocious grip. "Are you turning lamb on me now?"

"Let go!"

"You'll scare it away!" In a more genial tone, he whispered, "I would hate to think my Youth was a coward."

"You know I'm no coward, Stevens."

The redhead released his arm. "I've had too many disappoint-ments this summer."

"I won't disappoint you," Jake murmured.

The redhead patted his cheek, the touch brutal enough to feel more like a slap. "I was afraid my first time shooting a deer too."

"I told you, I'm not afraid," he insisted.

A doe approached the stream, gingerly at first, then more boldly. It bent its head toward the water, and Stevens whispered, "Kneel and get as steady as you can."

Jake's knee cracked as he knelt, his breath catching in the wind.

"Shoot the front shoulder or low in the stomach," the man continued. "Not the head or neck."

Jake raised his rifle, feeling it digging into his shoulder like the claws of a clinging animal.

"Fire!" Stevens hissed.

The gun flailed from side to side.

"Get a firm grip on it!"

The redhead's command made the doe's head rise. Jake felt his finger press against the trigger. The doe collapsed just as a piercing cry reverberated through the silent woods.

Stevens' shining eyes fell on him. "Right through the heart!"

"What was that scream?" Jake's throat tightened.

"What scream?"

"You heard it!" he shouted. "It sounded human!"

"Impossible!" the man insisted. "No one is here but us."

"In the trees. Oh, my God!"

Stevens crossed the stream, his step ripping through the shallow waters. He disappeared among the green leaves and wildflowers, and it seemed a long time before he emerged. His dark eyes were scorched with horror.

"It's all right."

Jake rushed forward. What he saw was not another hunter, as he expected, but the features of a boy not much older than Pines. The boy's hair stood wildly around his dirty face. His clothes were soiled and ragged, his arms and legs scratched like those of a runaway or an adventurer. He lay still and final like the lion skin on the floor of the trophy room.

CHAPTER 31

*J*ake saw nothing but a grim vision before him. He stumbled over thick vegetation, feeling Stevens' powerful hands on his elbows trying to steady him. He looked at the man's face through slitted eyes, despising his wordless pity.

"We must keep calm." The redhead spoke in his usual mild voice, "We must decide."

"Decide?" Jake growled. "'I ought to have waited. But you said not to wait. Shoot the moment you see it. You don't wait, but shoot."

"It was hardly our fault he was there," Stevens insisted.

"Not our fault, *my* fault." He looked at the man. "I don't ask you to take responsibility."

"Don't be a fool, man!" The calm in the redhead's tone dissolved.

Jake flung him away, "Leave me alone!"

"He ought to have called out," Stevens continued. "He must have heard us, even if we didn't hear him."

"He was a boy!" Jake screamed. "Just a boy!"

"A vagabond, most likely. A ruffian."

"So his life is worth nothing?" Jake pressed the collar of his coat around to his neck. He was suddenly freezing. "Maybe he's still breathing—"

Stevens placed a heavy hand on his shoulder. "He's quite dead, friend."

Jake collapsed, holding the man's arm. "Lord, Lord, what have I done?"

"You've done nothing," said the redhead. "And you'll do nothing. It's in my hands."

"Yes, you would say that." Jake glared at him. "'That each man shall take part in hunting parties organized by the Order, and that each Youth shall let his Patriarch guide him in the development of his strength, aggression, pride, and self-control.'" He choked out a laugh. "You've done your duty, Stevens. You've certainly encouraged the development of my strength and aggression."

"You've had a nasty shock, friend," The redhead lamented.

"Don't call me 'friend'!" Jake shouted. "I'm not your friend. I never was. I was a foolish young man looking for a father." His voice wheezed almost like his grandfather's last words. "What words of wisdom have you for a murderer?"

The redhead cleared his throat. "You really ought to get hold of yourself, Jake. You're not thinking clearly."

"I have you, my false father, to think for me."

"Clear thinking is a sign of a dignified man," Stevens continued.

"Another of Mr. Roosevelt's ideals, or perhaps Thoreau?" Jake asked. "Is killing an innocent boys as excusable as Mr. Roosevelt's casualties of war? Would Thoreau call it a sign of basic instinct? I think not!" He choked. "No, I think not!"

Stevens' eyes were burning. He said coldly, "If you'll calm down, I'll tell you of my solution."

Jake glared. "I have no choice, do I, my false father?"

"Not if you want me to save your neck!" This made Jake sag

against the wax wood tree. "No one knows we're here," Stevens said. "If we leave as quickly as possible, other hunters will find the boy."

"We can't leave him like that!"

In his dispassionate manner, the redhead answered, "We have a choice under the circumstances."

Jake's eyes clouded. "I see. 'The secrecy of the Order and its activities shall be maintained at all times.'"

"At *all* times."

"Including secrecy from the Order itself?" Jake asked. "That is what you're proposing, isn't it?"

"They can hardly be responsible," Stevens pointed out. "They weren't here."

"I told you, *I'm* responsible!"

"I must share the burden," said the redhead.

"I absolve you from your duty!" Jake held his arms high above his head. "I absolve you from it all, including this farcical paternity!"

Loons broke the silence of the woods, amassing in the blazing sky. The man's features lost their harness, and wariness sunk in. Stevens looked twenty years younger but twenty years wiser. "It was no farce, Jake."

"We spoke of mendacity, remember?" asked Jake. "It comes from the whole heart, you said."

"My heart spoke the truth, and it still does," said the man.

"Because you believe it," said Jake. "I no longer do." He turned from him.

They were silent for a while, the morning haze biting the air. "I can steer the Actaeons clear of this part of the woods," Stevens said. "They won't be the ones to discover it."

"Why do you say 'it'? The boy was a human being!" Jake screeched again.

"No one will discover the body for weeks," the redhead continued. "That ought to give us enough time."

"Time?"

"I have connections," said Stevens. "I'll give you money to take a boat out of the country."

"Sailing for where?"

The man's lips twisted into a smile. "Anywhere you wish."

Jake's hand melted into the wood. "Is that the Actaeon way with fugitives who threaten the sacredness of the Order? Out of sight, out of mind?"

"It was all a terrible mistake." The redhead's voice shook. "An accident."

Jake stumbled, the tree's spiked leaves falling over his shoulder. "Yes, that's right, isn't it? It was an accident. You were there, you saw it. The police will believe you."

"There's no need to go to the police if you go away," said Stevens.

"You told Vivian one must pay for a crime or a sin, like Actaeon paid for his crime of passion," Jake reminded him.

"This not a crime or a sin!"

"Call it a virtue, then," Jake said. "Even Teddy Roosevelt would agree, don't you think?" The smile felt bitter on his lips.

"Don't mock Roosevelt to me!" Stevens seethed. "He's twice the man you or I will ever be."

"I thought you agreed a young man ought to strive to be like him. 'That the manly virtues of restraint, grace, and morality upheld by our forefathers must be maintained and enhanced with power, aggression, and force.'"

"Stop mocking the principles of the Order!" The redhead gave him a vicious look.

"I have a right, don't I?" he said. "You're asking me to hide, to shirk away like a sloth under a rock."

"I am asking no such thing!"

"You forbade Maestro to run away from the salamanders," Jake said. "You spoke of courage." He let go of the tree, his feet unwavering for the first time that morning.

"This is about more than courage, and you damn well know it!"

"Vivian said something to me yesterday," he lamented. "I didn't understand then, but I do now."

The redhead took his arm. "Help me tie up the deer."

Jake backed away. "I'm going to the police."

"Then you go alone." Stevens' face froze with composure.

Jake felt the ice in his veins. "You won't stand by me?"

"The secrecy of the Order must be maintained."

"No one need know about the Order, Stevens," he said. "We say you and I went hunting alone. No one else was involved."

"You go alone," the man said carefully. "I shall deny everything."

Jake looked at him for a long time. The face remained as impassive as a mask. It was as if the terror of this man, whom he had looked upon as his guide, exonerated him from panic and despair. He was freed from the chains in which this false father had bound him. He was free.

He picked up the rifle. "You're a hard man to understand, Stevens."

"I never asked you to understand me," said the redhead. "I only asked you accept my instruction."

"I know," said Jake. "Perhaps my reasons for not doing so are stronger than yours were with Allcock."

The man looked at him with stone eyes. "What the devil do you mean?"

"I have no desire to rebel against anyone," he said.

"Rebel!"

"It was rather obvious." Jake smiled for the first time that morning. "Allcock was everything your father despised. Who better to guide you than his nemesis?"

They were still as the song of a bird rang over the trees, ending with a shriek as the bird flew off. Stevens' colossal figure looming like a steeple. "Recent events have confused you, Jake."

"Do you remember what my sister told you about the story of Actaeon?" His voice shook like the ringing of the loons. "Do you remember what she said about Actaeon's fate?"

"You need a drink." The redhead spoke in a hollow tone. "Shall we go back to camp and see if there is any of that rye left?"

"He was turned into a stag and devoured by those hounds he had trained so well."

"A consequence of Diana's distorted mind," Stevens snarled.

Jake grasped the rifle. "The result of his crime or sin, however you wish to call it. You might tell *that* to the Order. I don't think they know the whole story." He looked at the redhead over his shoulder. "Goodbye, Stevens. Good luck."

"I beg you to reconsider," the redhead murmured.

"I shall say nothing of you or the Order," he said. "That ought to reassure you."

Stevens flung the rifle away from Jake's arms and grabbed both his wrists. His control left him at last as his voice rose shrill and demonic in the sanctuary of trees. "You realize you'll be imprisoned. They may even hang you!"

A violent shiver ran down Jake's spine, but his voice was sober. "I don't think they'll hang me."

"You think they'll believe you when you tell them it was an accident?"

"Why shouldn't they believe me? I had nothing against the boy. I didn't even know him." He yanked himself out of the redhead's grip.

Stevens' tone changed to a note of appeal. "You shall disgrace your mother and sister."

He almost smiled. "My sister won't be disgraced once she learned I've done the right thing. And Mother — she'll survive this, as she's survived everything else." He pointed the tip of the gun at the man. "Your father would destroy you if you went to the police. He's the real reason you won't come with me, isn't it?"

Jake crossed the stream as the redhead shouted after him, "I'll deny everything. Remember that!"

"Every man must be left alone with his own conscience," said Jake to himself. "Only then he becomes a man." A light burned in his eyes, and he looked at the sun, feeling its warmth at last.

CHAPTER 32

*I*t took Jake a long time to get back to the hotel. He let instinct guide him back the way he and Vivian had gone the day he painted Diana with her crown of thorns. When he had descended the hill, he looked behind him, staring at the wax wood trees. They looked like overgrown mushrooms, the gaps in their bark a million eyes watching him — the eyes of Ancestor Hall, waiting to deliver their judgment upon him.

The afternoon sun warmed the Waxwoodian's red shingles and massive swirls. He stood looking at it for a moment, struck by its grandeur. *Grab at the stars, boy, before the moon's fire burns them down!* Those words had come to him when he had lingered over Grandfather's grave. He laughed, his body rocking. Stars, moon, fire. *Fire! Fire! Fire!* Stevens' voice roared against the rolling waves. He covered his ears. An elderly couple gave him an odd look.

The lobby was filled with people and baggage just as it had been the day he arrived. He imagined more than heard people tell droll anecdotes about summer adventures. They spoke freely, taking it for granted their secrets were safe with strangers, just as he had done with Stevens in the smoking car coming to

Waxwood. Was it then the redhead conceived of the idea of baiting him for the Actaeons?

A figure appeared through a bleary veil. "Are you all right, Jake?" The widow peered at him with magnified eyes. "You look like your world has just crumbled around you."

"Perhaps it has," he murmured.

He rushed past her up the stairs to the suite. Furnishings were in disarray, open trunks and suitcases lay on the floor and couch, and clothes were spread all around. The balcony doors were open, and he could see Vivian gazing out to the blue line of sea.

He let out a gasp. She stepped into the room. "You're back early." She examined him more closely. "What's wrong?"

Larissa emerged with a satin dress draped over her arm. "I thought you told me you would be gone all weekend," she said idly. "It's good you're here, though. You've plenty of time to pack."

"Mother." He could hardly get the words out. "Do you love me?" His heart was beating through his chest. "Do you?"

The dress fell from her hands, and she bent down to retrieve it, folding it neatly. "That's a rather childish question, Jacob."

"Do you!"

"I love you as every mother loves her son," she insisted.

"Do you believe I always try to do the right thing?"

"I would hope both you and your sister would always do the right thing." Her eyes slid toward Vivian.

His sister was at his side. "What did that foul man do to you?"

"Vivian!" Larissa's voice was piercing.

He grasped his mother's shoulders. "Mother, I'm a killer."

A scream escaped Vivian. Larissa remained composed even looked a little irritated. "I thought you gave up those boyish tales of yours a long time ago."

"No, I'm not a boy," he said. "But I killed one this morning." His voice rose. "I killed a boy in the woods. I was aiming for a doe, and the boy was hiding in the trees. I didn't look. I ought to have looked." His mind was spinning. "I'm like Actaeon now, you see." His voice pounded like a hammer against a stone wall. "The hunter turned into the hunted."

Larissa's refined features was no longer smooth. Wrinkles appeared around her eyes and lips. "Perhaps you'd better explain," she said quietly.

The story he told left out the Order, as he had promised. "I came back only to tell you I'm going to the police and take my punishment, whatever it may be."

"That scoundrel!" Vivian snarled.

A gust of wind raked his mother's hair, letting go of a few blond strands. "You will do no such thing." Both he and Vivian stared at her. "You will take Mr. Stevens' generous offer."

"You want me to run away?" Jake asked. "You can't mean it, Mother."

"For the sake of the family, I think it best."

"No!" Vivian's voice rang through the room like the loons that morning.

"I told you from the beginning that I expected you to make a contribution to the family." His mother's voice was steel. "I will not let you contribute by disgracing it."

"Disgracing what, Mother?" his sister's voice rattled through the suite. "The Alderdice family honor has been counterfeit from the beginning."

"This is not the time for your circle talk, Vivian," Larissa snapped.

"This is exactly the time!" His sister's hands grasping the edge of the couch. "Those faces in Ancestor Hall, the ones Jake found so comforting as a child, are nothing but strangers!"

His mother's lips quivered.

"Grandmother told me all about it." She looked at him. "It began when Grandfather passed an antique shop and saw a painting in the window. He thought it looked rather like him so he bought it. Thus Ancestor Hall was born!"

"Your grandmother had no right to tell you that!"

"He started gathering paintings of other men who looked like they might be ancestors," Vivian continued. "He made up all those stories he told you about them. He hated his own family, so he created a new one."

Jake said slowly, "You mean Great Uncle Floyd, and the judge, and the baron—"

She laid her hand in his. "All imposters. Except for Great-Grandfather and Grandfather, of course. And Grandmother, praise be, the only woman with guts enough to stand the truth!"

"He lied to us." His hands shook.

"He was afraid of anyone knowing he was a false prophet," Vivian hissed. "Even his own grandson."

"Vivian!" Larissa shrieked.

"His father was a drunkard, and his mother was a shrew. His brothers were parasites grabbing onto him for food and shelter and giving nothing back but their insolence. One can hardly build a family legacy out of that, can one?"

Jake sank into the nearest chair. "Is all this true, Mother?"

"What does it matter?"

"It matters!" he shouted. "I can't pretend it doesn't matter anymore."

Larissa was silent for a time, tending to a shawl on the couch with loving care. "He wanted you to aspire to something."

"More false fathers," he lamented. "How ironic. How terrible and ironic." His eyes closed, his forehead splitting with the names of all the false fathers: *Malcolm, Stevens, Great Uncle Floyd, Lorimar, Smith…*

He felt Vivian's hands on his shoulders. "It's better to know, isn't it?"

"Yes," he said. "It's better when one turns on the light in another's dark room." A wave of anger made him wrench free from her grasp. "I wish I had gone with you to Brandywine that day. I wish I had!"

"What are you talking about?" His mother glared at him.

"After Grandmother's funeral," he said, "When Viv disobeyed you and went to Waxwood. I went with her."

Her face turned pale. "My God, Vivian, he was only fifteen!"

"He came back on the train, didn't he?" Vivian said sharply. "He didn't go to Brandywine with me." In a softer tone, she added, "Now I'm glad he didn't."

"Glad?" He looked. at her.

"You were so young, Jake," she said. "You still are."

"Not after today." He gave a strange laugh. "I'm well ripened for anything after today." His eyes fell on Larissa. "Mother, how could you go on with that farce for so many years?"

"I wanted to give you a past filled with virtue and dignity," she said. "Is that so wrong?"

"I'm sorry if I'm hurting you, Mother," said Jake. "But not knowing the truth hurts more. I know that now too."

His mother's eyes mirrored the persecuting gaze of Ancestor Hall. The damning verdict he had been waiting for was in, but it came not from those ghosts, but from someone very much alive.

The distress looming like a storm finally broke, and tears choked him. "For God's sake! If you ever loved me, help me!"

"I'm trying to help you." She sat down at the desk. "I don't think we should involve Mr. Stevens now, though his offer was kind."

"Kind!" Vivian spit out. "He was trying to save his own skin."

Larissa shot her the warning look. With steady hands, she scribbled on a check and held it out to him. Her voice wavered as she said, "I'll send you more when you let me know where you are."

"That's your idea of helping me?" He wailed.

"For God's sake, what do you expect me to do?" she shrieked.

Jake couldn't see his sister now. He saw only Larissa holding out the check, her expression closing the lid over him like a coffin. He was being put aside as another family Unmentionable.

He rose. "It's not for you to do anything. It's for me. As head of the family, I must do the right thing."

"I'm glad you're being sensible."

"I mean *right*," he said. "Do you know what *right* is, Mother?"

"There is hardly the time—"

"Let him speak." His sister' said. "For once, let him speak!"

"Right is having the courage to face one's fears," he said. "A man must achieve that on his own. No false father can give it to him. Nor a mother." He looked at her for a long time. She turned away, her hand still clutching the check.

"If that is your decision," she said, "you can't expect us to abide by it."

"I abide by it!" Vivian screeched.

"I don't expect it," said Jake. "I shall not see either of you again, if that's what you want."

His sister rushed toward him, but he held her back.

"You're willing to pay that price?" Larissa asked in a quiet voice.

"Some things are worth more than family honor, Mother."

She looked at him. "You are indeed no longer a child, Jacob."

"You'll wish me luck, at least?" He held out his hand.

She grasped both his shoulders. For the first time since he could remember, there was something almost tender in her touch. She whispered, "Take care of yourself."

He turned to his sister. "Viv—" But when she stepped toward him, her face stained with tears, he couldn't bear to look at her or have her touch him. He could only mumble a vague promise to write and stumble out of the suite.

He held himself steady with the maturity and wisdom all who had taken a piece of his life had denied him. He imagined future Alderdices led by the hand through Alderdice Hall looking upon his portrait, saying, *"He went to prison because he did what he thought was right."* It would not be brilliant or dignified but at least it would be the truth.

. . .

~~~~~

Author's Note

Hello, reader! Thank you for reading Book 2 of the Waxwood Series. I hope you enjoyed Jake's journey to manhood and his struggle to define the meaning of the word in the rapidly changing Gilded Age.

I will be honest: I'm a woman's writer. That is, I feel more comfortable writing about women characters than male characters. It was a struggle for me to write about a young man's coming-of-age from a man's point of view.

So why did I? First, Jake is an important member of the Alderdice family, as you've seen. He is, as his mother points out, the next generation patriarch. Second, his relationship with his mother is as complicated as Vivian's but in a very different way. And third, I wanted to show the male side of the Gilded Age and how gender expectations (which figure so prominently in Vivian's story) also affected young men during this time. It wasn't only women who were redefining their roles and shifting their views on who they were but men as well.

I ended up enjoying writing Jake's story and many readers have told me how much they really love this character. My editor called his story "heartbreaking". Although the series continues with Vivian's story, you'll hear more about Jake and about another character in this book later on in the series.

. . .
~~~~~

In Book 3, we return to Vivian. But this is a different Vivian than the one you met in Book 1 (and if you haven't met her yet, I encourage you to download *The Specter* and read that book — it's free in all online bookstores!) She's on the path to enlightenment, though the path isn't always very bright or pleasant. Turn the page to read an excerpt from the book!

Happy reading!
    Tam

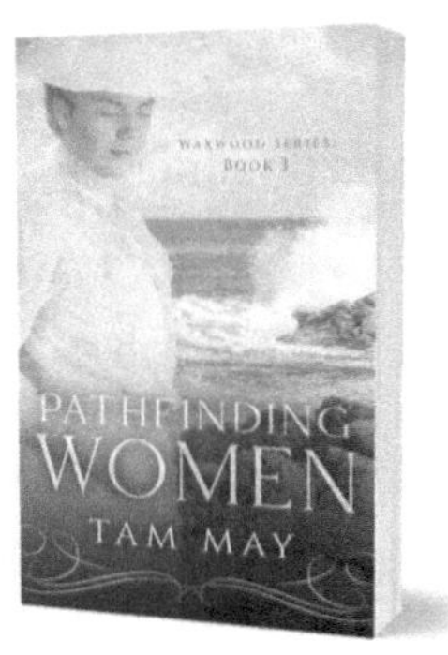

Waxwood, 1899: Vivian Alderdice is twenty-six, unmarried, and has no prospective suitors. Her brother's tragic plight the year before left the family on shaky ground in Nob Hill society. Their social position depends on Vivian capturing the heart of a wealthy Canadian bachelor determined to become a member of their exclusive society. But to win him, she and her mother must spend the summer in Waxwood.

Waxwood brings back memories of Vivian searching for her grandmother's identity and uncovering family secrets she wasn't prepared to deal with, but she's determined to leave all that behind her.

Then a young man she meets on the train brings those skeletons out of the closet again, and Vivian finds herself torn between her fulfilling her social obligations or tracing a past that might lead to uncovering more family secrets.

Will Vivian's summer unravel family truths that might destroy her family forever? Or will those months unearth a more authentic version of herself and where she stands as the new century approaches?

"This is a fascinating read!"

Read on for an excerpt from this book!

They did not see the Griffiths or the Tishers as they made their way through the crowds to the elevators, a hotel porter lagging behind with their suitcases. As they entered, she stole a glance at her mother. The bony structure that had always stood out as aristocratic was embossed with the hardness of one who had seen more than her share of burdens.

"Are you all right, Mother?" she asked in a tender voice.

Larissa sighed. "I suppose I'm a little tired." She patted Vivian's hand. "We'll rest before dinner, and I'll be all right." They squeezed past people as they got out at their floor.

From the stairwell, two figures appeared. Both were men dressed in plaid suits with slightly ruffled shirt fronts and both had broad foreheads and square features that stood out distinctly on their faces. One was older than the other, so they were clearly father and son, the father looking to be in his sixties and the son twenty years or so younger. They spoke in hushed voices, but their somewhat twangy tones carried down the long hallway.

As they came toward her and Larissa, Vivian caught the lingering bright eyes regarding them with an open stare that was not quite lurid but not as discreet as it might be. The men gave a slight bow in their direction and, without waiting for her and Larissa to return it, continued down to the other end of the hall, silent now.

"Well, that was fresh, wasn't it?" Vivian said with a laugh.

Her mother pulled her to the suite where their luggage was already waiting for them outside their suite. "Your observations are rather dim in some quarters, Vivian."

"I don't understand." She fished into her bag for the extra room key the hotel clerk had given her.

"I believe we have just had our first encounter with the Leblancs."

Vivian eyed her. "How do you know?"

"I don't," her mother confessed. "I only have a feeling."

She played with the key in her hand. "So that's the catch of the season, is it? He looked more like a dragoon than a buccaneer."

"He looked like neither," said her mother sternly. "I thought they were quite cultured."

"Is the father looking for a wife too?" Vivian grinned. "He certainly took as much interest in us as his son when they passed."

"Vivian, don't be vulgar!"

They entered the suite just as the porter appeared with apologies for abandoning the baggage and brought each piece into the rooms under Larissa's firm guidance.

It was only after he was gone that Vivian got a look at the suite. Her heart turned cold. "Mother, we can't stay here!"

"Why ever not?" Her mother unpinned her hat and straightened her hair.

Her tongue felt dry. "Don't you see?" Her voice came out in a croak.

It was clear her mother did not see. She didn't see the silver panels where spots that had been chipped by careless past inhabitants were painted over smoothly. She didn't see that the painting on the wall was a John Singer-Sargent, looking just as faded as it had the year before.

"We were here last year!" she burst out. "Exactly in this room."

"Vivian, you have got to stop feeling that everything points toward the past." Her mother's voice was firm. "We're looking to the future now."

Vivian thought about the two men they had just passed. They looked amiable and, despite the lingering eyes, cultured, as her mother had said. The open face of the younger one, even though she had seen it for only a moment, appealed to her, and even their freshness had a bold honesty to it. And yet, she felt afraid. It was as if a man in a portrait had come to life and now, she would be forced to speak to him, take his arm, perhaps more. And then he would take her back into the portrait with him, and she would be trapped inside the gilded frame, the box folding over her like those knitted faces in Alderdice Hall. Only she would still be alive.

Will Vivian be trapped inside the past or will she be freed of it? You can find out by purchasing a copy of *Pathfinding Women* at your favorite online bookstore at this link: https:// tammayauthor.com/books-2/waxwood-series/pathfinding-women-waxwood-series-book-3.

How about that cool freebie I promised you? If you're into historical cozy mysteries featuring strong women who don't let society's rules about female behavior stop them from doing what they want, I urge you to check out the Adele Gossling Mysteries! Read on for how to get hold of the series' free novella, *The Missing Ruby Necklace*.

When a jewel and a girl go missing on New Year's Eve...

Eleanor McCarthy, a lovely though somewhat flighty debutante, has graced the tiny town of Arrojo, California, with her presence. One of Arrojo's prominent ladies throws a New Year's Eve shindig to introduce her to Arrojo's high society — whatever little of it there is. Naturally, the daughter and son of one of San

Francisco's influential lawyers, Adele and Jackson Gossling, are invited.

But screams replace popping champagne corks when Eleanor's priceless ruby necklace is discovered missing. And soon, so is Eleanor!

In this historical cozy mystery set in the early 20th century, follow Adele Gossling, stationary store owner and amateur sleuth, and her clairvoyant sidekick Nin Branch as they search for a ruby necklace that may or may not have been stolen and a young woman who may or may not have run away.

Want to read an excerpt from this book? I got you covered! Turn the page.

"Coffee!" Miss McCarthy laughed. "Heavens, no! I haven't had my first taste of champagne yet." She flung her hand out to her brother. "Bring me a bottle of champagne, my good man."

"I don't mind," he said.

Before he could saunter out the door, Mrs. Abberton jumped up. "I'll get it."

"I really think we ought to get coffee," Mr. Abberton mumbled.

"She wants champagne," Mrs. Abberton was almost stern. "It's a celebration, after all!" She practically fled from the room.

Adele followed her and caught her arm. She spoke in a soft tone. "Mrs. Abberton, why did Miss McCarthy faint?"

"She just told you, didn't she?" The woman gave a shrill laugh. "Albert said we ought to open some windows, but it was such a windy night, I —"

"It wasn't the windows," said Adele. "Or the corset."

"Of course it was!" The woman examined some bottles on the floor. "I never could read these labels."

"You were staring at Miss McCarthy as if something that wasn't there."

"What an imagination you have, dear." The woman said.

"Miss McCarthy had her hands on her throat when she fell," Adele continued. "You kept looking at her throat."

"Nonsense," the woman hissed.

"Miss McCarthy wasn't wearing her ruby necklace," Adele declared.

Mrs. Abberton tore through a row of bottles lying on a table. One rolled onto the floor with a crack and the bubbly drink spilled across the marble. She sunk into one of the chairs. "You're too observant, Miss Gossling."

"You saw it too."

"Just before the lights went out," she said. "But Eleanor is one of those girls who gets easily flustered with her jewelry. She says it weighs her down."

"If that's true, why were you so alarmed just now?" Adele said.

"I wasn't," the woman insisted. "She locks that necklace in a box. Albert tried to persuade her to put it in our safe at the finance company, but she refused."

"That's rather unusual," Adele said.

"Eleanor's a lovely girl, but rather flighty," The woman said in a harsh tone. "I expect Celestine spoils her."

"If the necklace is missing, there might be a theft involved," Adele suggested.

Jewelry goes missing all the time. But does that mean theft? And why is Mrs. Abberton so nervous?

How can you get your hands on a copy of *The Missing Ruby Necklace*, not available in any bookstore? Simple. Go to this link: https://landing.mailerlite.com/webforms/landing/ l2u0c3. What else will you get when you get this novella? How about fun facts about women in history and true crime classic mysteries, which are just as fascinating, if not more so, as contemporary true crimes?

Writing has been Tam May's voice since the age of fourteen. She writes stories about powerful women set in the past. Her fiction gives readers a sense of justice for women, both the living and the dead. Tam's stories are set mostly around the Bay Area because she adores sourdough bread, Ghirardelli chocolate, and San Francisco history.

Tam is the author of the Adele Gossling Mysteries which take place in the early 20th century and features sassy suffragist and epistolary expert Adele Gossling whose talent for solving crimes doesn't sit well with the ideas of some people around her about women's place. Tam has also written historical fiction about women breaking loose from the confinements of their era.

Although Tam left her heart in San Francisco, she lives in the Midwest because it's cheaper. When she's not writing, she's devouring everything classic (books, films, art, music) and concocting yummy vegan dishes.

Tam May can be reached at:
WEBSITE: http://tammayauthor.com/
EMAIL: tammay70@tammayauthor.com
FACEBOOK: https://www.facebook.com/tammayauthor
INSTAGRAM: https://www.instagram.com/tammayauthor/
PINTEREST: https://www.pinterest.com/tammayauthor/